Magicians, sorcerers, w......., necromancers, whichever name you use for them, it has a thrilling magical ring to it, and so have the stories in this book. Every one of them has a magician in it, be he good or bad, clever, clumsy, kindly or downright malicious, and of course plenty of the most exciting magic goes with them.

There's the strange story of Merlin, our national magician you might call him, who watched over the young King Arthur, most glorious of all our kings, and sleeps now, waiting till his country needs him again. There's the well-known magician 'uncle' who was such an enemy to Aladdin, and other less familiar tales about the sorcerer Polyidus, who found the little dead prince Glaucus where he was hidden in the palace at Knossos, and of the maiden Bradamante (a medieval exponent of Women's Lib if ever there was one), who, armed as a knight, sallied forth with Magic Ring and Magic Shield to find her lost lover Roger.

There's a sad tale by Mrs Ewing of a magician godfather who gave his princely godson one of the most tragic, unexpected of all christening gifts, Rudyard Kipling's story of the Crab who defied the Eldest Magician of all when he created the animals, and E. Nesbit's romantic tale of the young princess in an enchanted tower set in a stormy sea, and the great kind clever cat that looked after her ... in fact, this book is a real enchantment of enchanters. Read it, and you will forget all else. It's magic, you see.

A BOOK OF
MAGICIANS

EDITED BY
ROGER LANCELYN GREEN

ILLUSTRATED BY
VICTOR AMBRUS

PUFFIN BOOKS
in association with Hamish Hamilton
Children's Books Ltd

Puffin Books, Penguin Books Ltd, Harmondsworth, Middlesex, England
Penguin Books, 625 Madison Avenue, New York, New York 10022, U.S.A.
Penguin Books Australia Ltd, Ringwood, Victoria, Australia
Penguin Books Canada Ltd, 2801 John Street, Markham, Ontario, Canada L3R 1B4
Penguin Books (N.Z.) Ltd, 182–190 Wairau Road, Auckland 10, New Zealand

—

First published by Hamish Hamilton Children's Books Ltd 1973
Published in Puffin Books 1977
Reprinted 1978

—

Copyright © Roger Lancelyn Green, 1973
Illustrations copyright © Victor Ambrus, 1973
All rights reserved

—

Made and printed in Great Britain by
Richard Clay (The Chaucer Press) Ltd
Bungay, Suffolk
Set in Monotype Bembo

Believe, then, if you please, that I can do strange things: I have, since I was three year old, conversed with a Magician, most profound in his art, and yet not damnable.

Shakespeare

Contents

Introduction

THE *Oxford English Dictionary* tells us simply that a Magician is 'One skilled in magic or sorcery; a necromancer, wizard': but we all have our own picture of the ideal Magician who comes immediately to mind when that Word of Power is uttered.

It has probably always been so. Every primitive tribe of savages in the jungles of long ago had its Magician: but perhaps he was not as great and awe-inspiring as the Magician whom the oldest member of the tribe could remember from when he was a boy . . . Indeed, there are still magicians in the remotest corners of the world: I met one the other day in the jungles of far Peru, 'on the banks of the turbid Amazon'. There was a white magician living not far away, whom we could simply call a Doctor: but if he failed in his cures, the Witch Doctor of the tribe turned to magic to help his people.

For a Magician really means a wise man, one who knows more than the general run of people. The Magi who followed the wonderful Star which led them to Bethlehem were Magicians, for Mage is but another variant of the word. And, as they came from the East, they were thought to be wiser than the people of Palestine: for wisdom dwelt in the East, and Babylonians were thought to be the greatest magicians in the world.

Ur of the Chaldees is in Babylonia, and Abraham came from it in search of the Promised Land. His descendant, Moses, was the greatest Magician of Israel, and he defeated Pharaoh's magicians in the Land of Egypt, though the Egyptians had another version of the story and are the earliest people whose tales of magic have come down to us.

As people grew more civilized their attitude to Magicians

began to change. Magicians were not so common, but were much wiser when they did exist – if they really existed at all. The ancient Greeks were not very sure about it, and there are few Greek myths in which magic plays a part – and their later writers tend to treat magicians as pure fancy – as Lucian did. And even witches were already little more than useful characters for fiction . . . though one feels that Apuleius, who wrote about them in his *Golden Ass* at much the same time, was not at all sure, and wanted to be on the safe side . . .

It was in the Middle Ages, when the Romances of Chivalry were being written – tales of King Arthur and Charlemagne, Huon of Bordeaux and Bevis of Southampton – that Magicians really came into their own, and of them all Merlin was the most famous and appears in the greatest number of tales:

> I command you to remember
> Arthur's court and me, Merlin,
> Master of all men there . . .

The end of the Middle Ages was also the period when Black Magic was greatly feared. A Black Wizard had sold his soul to the Devil in return for his magic powers – and deserved to be burnt at the stake. Some of them really tried to gain power and long life by these means: there was Giles de Retz, for example, who began as a Marshal of France and a friend of Joan of Arc, and ended by sacrificing children to the Devil in an attempt to regain his youth. His deeds were so atrocious that out of them grew the story of Blue Beard; but the would-be wizard Giles makes his most memorable appearance in S. R. Crockett's romance *The Black Douglas* (1899).

An even more famous Magician, a real man who became a legend, was Dr John Faustus about whom both Marlowe and Goethe wrote plays and Gounod an opera. Even early scientists and inventors like Roger Bacon and Cornelius Agrippa and Dr Dee were apt to be classed as Magicians and had to be very careful what they did and said – and able to prove that they used no magic.

But the same period was producing such great narrative poems as Ariosto's *Orlando Furioso* and Spenser's *Faerie Queene* full of marvels and Magicians, magic spells, Dragons, fairy princesses, and all the rest of it. And a century later fairy tales began to be written down, and fairy tales invented by the ladies of the Court of Louis XIV of France – and the Magician of Fiction had, once and for all, ousted the real Mages: though their distant cousins are still with us in various disguises ranging from Spiritualist mediums to psychoanalysts.

The earlier stories in this *Book of Magicians* give examples of most kinds of wizards from the ancient Egyptians to the Medieval and chivalric; and also of the more powerful Magicians of Fairy Tale and Folklore. When literary invention begins, the choice becomes more difficult. There are Magicians and Sorcerers, Wizards and Necromancers of all sorts playing larger or smaller parts in full-length stories: but I have not tried to make extracts, since it has always seemed to me that to do so spoils the enjoyment when one comes to read the whole book – besides usually proving unsatisfactory in itself.

But I hope that the Magicians in this volume may encourage readers to set out in quest of other workers of magic more fully described elsewhere. And there is a bounteous crop from which to choose. If there are few good stories of the Magicians of actual savage folklore, there are excellent and authentic Wizards to be found, for example, in Rider Haggard's romances of Zululand a century ago, from the great Zikali in *Child of Storm* and *Finished* to Indabazimbi in *Allan's Wife* and Hokosa, the hero of *The Wizard*. There is one of the greatest Wizards of romance, Gandalf the Grey, in J. R. R. Tolkien's *The Hobbit* and *The Lord of the Rings*; and very fine wicked Magicians in John Masefield's *The Midnight Folk* and *The Box of Delights*, not to mention the splendid Snagaraguus in that undeservedly forgotten 'fairy thriller' *Josephine* by Geoffrey Mure, and my own Black Wizard in *The Land of the Lord High Tiger*. And there are Magicians who live in the modern world like J. B. S. Haldane's *My Friend Mr Leakey*, or come into it like my *Wonderful Stranger* or, best of all, have a foot in more worlds than one like the splendid Magicians in C. S. Lewis's *The Voyage of 'The Dawn Treader'* and *The Magician's Nephew*.

But there are heaps more in books both earlier and later – and by now most of you are probably saying, with A. A. Milne's Woodcutter: 'In realms of Fairylore I need no guide nor tutor.' And, though I cannot end by waving a magic wand and transporting you into the very Lands of Enchantment, I can at least invite you, like Tennyson's young mariner, to follow the Gleam that shines from it:

> Oh young Mariner,
> You that are watching
> The gray Magician
> With eyes of wonder ...
> The Master whispered
> 'Follow the Gleam!'

Invitation

The Sorcerer's Song

W. S. GILBERT

Oh! my name is John Wellington Wells –
I'm a dealer in Magic and Spells,
   In blessings and curses,
   And ever-filled purses,
In prophecies, witches and knells!
If you want a proud foe to 'make tracks' –
If you'd melt a rich uncle in wax –
   You've but to look in
   On our resident Djinn,
Number seventy, Simmery Axe.

We've a first class assortment of Magic;
   And for raising a posthumous shade
With effects that are comic or tragic,
   There's no cheaper house in the trade.
Love-philtre – we've quantities of it;
   And for knowledge if any one burns,
We keep an extremely small prophet
   Who brings us unbounded returns!

My name is John Wellington Wells,
I'm a dealer in Magic and Spells,
   In blessings and curses,
   And ever-filled purses –
In prophecies, witches and knells.
If anyone anything lacks,
He'll find it all ready in stacks,
   If he'll only look in
   On our resident Djinn,
Number seventy, Simmery Axe!

PART ONE
Magicians of Ancient Days

Teta the Magician

NEARLY five thousand years ago, when the Pharaoh Khufu reigned in Egypt, the building of his Great Pyramid at Giza was begun. His architect, Hemon, had learnt all the wisdom of Imhotep who had built the Step Pyramid for Zoser a hundred years before, and the people of Egypt turned out in their thousands during the months of the Inundation each year when no farming was possible, and laboured gladly to the glory of the good god Pharaoh Khufu – who, like all true Pharaohs of Egypt, was held to be an incarnation of the spirit of the god Amen-Ra himself.

But there was one thing lacking. Hemon and the magicians of Memphis could not find the papyrus roll on which Imhotep was said to have written the words of power to keep a pyramid safe for ever against earthquake and thunderbolt – the weapons of Set the evil one.

So Khufu sent out messengers and offered rewards to any who could find the words of power. The priests in the temples, from Philae to Tanis, searched their records; the magicians of Thebes and Abydos and Heliopolis sought the aid of spells and incantations – but all in vain.

At last, however, one of Pharaoh's sons, the Prince Hordedef, came to his father and bowing to the ground, said:

'Pharaoh my father – life, health, strength be to you – I have found a magician stronger and more wonderful than any in your realm. His name is Teta and he dwells not far hence, at Meidum near the pyramid of your father Seneferu. There is no one like him in all Egypt: he is a man of one hundred and ten years old, and was a boy when Zoser reigned and Imhotep built the first pyramid – and he eats five hundred bread-cakes and a side of beef, and drinks one hundred draughts of beer each day, even now. He knows how to restore the head that is smitten off; he knows how to make the savage lion of the desert follow him like a tame dog dragging its leash behind it – and he swears that he knows how you may find the papyrus of Imhotep inscribed with the words of power and the charms that must be spoken to keep a pyramid safe from the blows of Set the evil one who would destroy the dwelling places of the dead if they were not protected.'

Khufu the Pharaoh was delighted at this news, and said: 'Go in person, Hordedef my son, and take with you the royal litter and many attendants. Bring Teta the magician hither to Memphis with all speed, and treat him as if he were a subject prince visiting me his lord. Sail up the Nile in the Royal Boat so that Teta may travel with ease and comfort.'

So Hordedef set out in the Royal Boat, taking with him all things needful. Up the river he went, beyond Saqqara, beyond the pyramids of Dahshur, until he came to the pyramid of Meidum built by Seneferu. Here he landed and set out up the royal causeway to the pyramid, and round it to the village beyond, where dwelt Teta the magician.

They found the old man lying on a couch of palmwood in the shade of his house, while his servants fanned him and anointed his head and feet with oil.

Prince Hordedef saluted him reverently, saying: 'Greetings worthy of your great and revered age be to you, Teta the magician, and may you continue free of the infirmities of the old. I come with a message from my father Khufu the great Pharaoh – life, health, strength be to him. He bids you visit him at Memphis and share of the best of food and wine even as he himself eats and drinks. Moreover, he has sent his own Royal Boat so that you may travel in ease and comfort; and here is the royal litter of ebony set with gold in which you shall be carried, even as Pharaoh himself is borne, from here down to the Royal Boat, and from it to the palace in Memphis.'

Then Teta the magician replied: 'Peace be with you, Hordedef, son of the great Pharaoh, beloved of your father! May Khufu the Pharaoh – life, health, strength be to him – advance you among his councillors and bring you all good things! May your *Ka* prevail against your enemies, and may your *Bai* find the road of righteousness that leads to the throne of Osiris in the Duat! I will come with you to the presence of Pharaoh. But let another boat follow bringing my attendants and the book of my art.'

All things were done as Teta desired, and in due time he

sailed down the Nile in the Royal Boat and was carried in the royal litter to the palace at Memphis.

When Khufu heard of Teta's arrival he cried: 'Bring him before me immediately!' So Teta was led into the Hall of Columns where Pharaoh awaited him on his throne with the great men of Egypt gathered about him.

Pharaoh said to Teta: 'How is it, mighty master of magic, that I have not seen you before?' And Teta answered: 'He who is summoned is he who comes. The good god Pharaoh Khufu – life, health, strength be to him – has sent for me, and behold I am here.'

Then Pharaoh said: 'Is it true, as I have heard tell, that you can restore to its place the head that is smitten off?'

And Teta replied: 'That indeed I can do, by the magic and wisdom of my hundred years and ten.'

'Bring from the prison one who is doomed to die,' commanded Khufu. 'And let the executioner come also to perform the death sentence on the criminal.'

But Teta exclaimed: 'Let it not be a man, oh Pharaoh my lord. Let it be ordered that the head be smitten from some other living creature.'

So a duck was brought into the Hall of Columns and its head was cut off and laid at one end while its body remained at the other. Then Teta spoke the rolling words of power, and at his secret charm the duck's body fluttered along the ground, and its head moved likewise until they came together. And when the two parts met they joined, and the duck stood flapping its wings and quacked loudly.

Then a goose was brought, and the same magic was performed. And when an ox was beheaded Teta had but to speak the great words of power that made up his charm and the dead ox rose lowing to its feet and followed him across the Hall of Columns with its halter trailing on the ground.

Then said Pharaoh: 'All that is reported of you is true, Teta, greatest of magicians. But now can you tell me that which I long to know: where lies the papyrus on which Imhotep wrote the words of power that went to the building of the pyramid for Zoser, yes and for that of Seneferu my father also.'

'I can tell you where the papyrus lies,' answered Teta. 'It is in a casket of flint that is hidden in the great temple of Thoth at Heliopolis. I cannot tell where that casket is concealed, but I know by my art that only one person can find that casket for you – yes, and I can tell you who it is.'

'Speak, then, greatest of magicians!' exclaimed Khufu eagerly. 'And great indeed shall be your reward.'

'This very night,' answered Teta, 'the wife of a priest at Heliopolis shall bear three children at a birth, and the spirit of Amen-Ra shall be in them. Her name is Rud-didet, and one of her children shall find the casket . . . One of her children shall also sit where you sit and rule over Egypt.'

Then Khufu's heart was troubled, and he said: 'Surely it would be better to send and slay Rud-didet ere ever her children are born. For only by treachery can one of them become Pharaoh of Egypt.'

But Teta said: 'Let not your heart be troubled. Your son Kafra shall reign after you, and Menkaura his son after him, before a son of Rud-didet sits on the throne of the Upper and Lower Land. The words of power can be found and spoken by none but he – and if he speaks them three great pyramids shall rise at Giza and stand there for ever. But if he speaks them not, all that you build, and your son builds and your son's son after him shall fall and crumble away and become as the sands of the desert.'

So Khufu issued a decree that the children of Rud-didet should dwell at Heliopolis in all honour, and that if any lifted a hand against them – be he a prince of Egypt – he should die a death of shame, and his body be destroyed so that his *Ka* should perish also. And he bade Hordedef take Teta the magician to dwell in his palace for the rest of his days, giving him daily a thousand bread-cakes, a hundred draughts of beer, a side of beef, and whatever else he might desire.

Meanwhile the three children of Rud-didet were born, and when the eldest User-kaf played in the temple of Amen-Ra as a boy he found the casket of flint in which was the papyrus roll containing the words of power. And, as a young priest, he read them at the dedication of the great pyramid of Khufu; as high priest of Heliopolis he read them at the dedication of the pyramid of Kafra, and as Pharaoh elect he read them at the dedication of the pyramid of Menkaura. And when Menkaura was laid in his pyramid, User-kaf became Pharaoh of all Egypt – the first Pharaoh of the Fifth Dynasty.

As for the words of power and the charm against Set the evil, they seem to have done all that Khufu the Pharaoh wished: for the three great pyramids of Khufu, Kafra and Menkaura stand at Giza to this day – the first of the Seven Wonders of the ancient world, and the only one that is still standing nearly five thousand years later.

A Hittite Charm against a Wizard's Spell

*The Priestess throws a thread into the fire
on the altar and sings:*

Just as I here have burnt this thread
    And it will not return,
So let the Wizard's curse be dead,
    Let his enchantments burn.

I vanquish thus his Words of Power,
    Thus die each charm of his;
The Wizard's power is burnt this hour –
    My spell more potent is.

I cast a double counter-spell,
    I spit upon his name,
I trample on his charms as well –
    The ass shall do the same.

Let all men spit upon them now
    And on the Wizard too:
Then all his spells shall end, I vow,
    Whatever he may do.

The Magician from Corinth

MORE than three thousand years ago, when Minos and Pasiphae were king and queen of Crete, there came to their court a magician from Greece whose name was Polyidus. This wise man had left his home in Corinth to see if he could add yet further to his wisdom in the great city of Knossos, and Minos made him Palace Magician and set him above all the wise men of Crete.

For a long time nothing occurred to test whether Polyidus was cleverer than the rest of the Cretan sages, until one day the little Prince Glaucus disappeared mysteriously.

In the great Palace at Knossos it was very easy for anyone to get lost – and indeed there were so many passages and stairways winding hither and thither that its name 'The Labyrinth' has ever since been given to any such maze as this.

At first Minos bade his guards search the Palace from top to bottom; and when they failed to find any sign of Glaucus, he sent for his own wise men and commanded them to discover by their arts what had become of his son.

The wise men consulted together and looked into their magic glasses. Then they came to Minos and said:

'O King, we cannot tell you where the Prince your son has gone. But we have seen mysterious things by our divining and this we know: "Today a strange creature has been born in your land, and the man who can best say what it is like is he who will find the Prince and restore him living to you." None of us can see further than this, nor unravel the riddle: but doubtless the stranger magician from Greece whom you have set over us can both read it and give you back your son.'

This they said as much out of jealousy towards Polyidus as because they themselves were still unable to find Glaucus.

When he heard their words Minos sent at once for the Greek Magician, and Polyidus came before him and before the other magicians; and when he had heard their words and looked into their hearts, he said:

'My lord King, this riddle is an easy one to read. It concerns a calf born not long ago in your royal herd which grazes near the sea, upon the hillside above Amnisos. This calf changes its colour during the day from white in the morning to red at noon and black in the evening. Of all things this most resembles the fruit on a mulberry tree – for when it first forms it is white in colour; then it turns red; but when it is ripe and ready to eat its colour is black.'

'This must surely be the true answer,' cried all the Cretan magicians in delight. 'This proves that Polyidus and no other can find Prince Glaucus and restore him living to your majesty.'

'Be it so,' answered Minos. 'Magician of Greece, prove to us that your skill is greater than that of all the wise men of Crete – and your reward shall be great in proportion. But if you fail, then we will know that you are but a cheat, and your punishment shall be great also.'

Polyidus was much concerned at this, and felt that the Cretan magicians had trapped him. But he only bowed to the King and said:

'My lord, give me time and let me wander about the Palace alone, and I will solve the riddle of the missing Prince just as I solved that of the mulberry-coloured calf.'

So Polyidus went up on to the roof of the Palace and looked to see if he could learn anything from the birds: for from their flight many things were to be discovered by a magician who knew how to interpret their prophecies.

Presently he saw a great sea-eagle come flying slowly and wearily to shore and settle on a tower above one corner of the Palace.

'Ah,' said Polyidus to himself, 'this surely means that the child is somewhere on dry land. If the eagle had flown away from land he would have been saying: "The thing you seek within the sea lies dead." But since he leaves his own home and the place where he finds his food, and comes to me on the land, he is saying: "The thing you seek lies not within the sea." So now I must search the Palace and see if any other bird will help me in my quest.'

Polyidus came down from the roof and wandered down the great staircase and by many a passage and hidden doorway until he came to the maze of storage cellars where food and wine was kept for all its many inhabitants.

Presently he found an owl sitting above the entrance to a stairway leading yet farther down.

'Ah,' said Polyidus, 'here is my next guide. "Glaux" means an owl in Greek, and Glaux will lead me to Glaucus.'

Sure enough, as he drew near the owl flew down from its perch and flapped its way into the lower cellar. After it came Polyidus, and presently found it sitting on the edge of a jar of honey, flapping its wings to drive away the flies.

Now the jars in the Palace of Knossos were as big as barrels, and sometimes higher than the tallest man; and this was one of the biggest, and it was full to the brim with liquid honey.

On top of the honey floated a ball – and at once Polyidus realized what had happened. Glaucus had followed his ball down into the cellar; it had bounced up into the great jar, and he had climbed after it, fallen into the honey, and been drowned.

Polyidus told the sad news to King Minos, and the body of the little Prince was taken out of the honey and placed in the royal tomb – a vault cut out in the rock and richly decorated in gold.

'And now,' said King Minos to Polyidus, 'You have found the body of my son which was lost; but you must also find his

spirit, which is lost too. My wise men said that whoever could solve the riddle of the mulberry-coloured calf could find Glaucus and restore him to me alive and well. Magician of Corinth, here indeed is your chance to prove your greatness in the arts of magic and to show that the wise men of Greece know more than those of Crete.'

'To bring the dead to life is no matter of wisdom – or of magic!' cried Polyidus perceiving the snare set for him by the Cretan wizards. 'It is against the will of Zeus, King of the Gods! Did he not slay with a thunderbolt Asclepius the son of Apollo for bringing to life the dead Hippolytus?'

'Nevertheless you must risk the anger of Zeus – or die your-self!' cried Minos. 'Guards! Place Polyidus the Greek Magician in the tomb with my son, and shut them in with the great slab of stone that fits over the entrance. But keep watch outside so that you can release both of them when Glaucus is restored to life.'

So Polyidus was lowered into the tomb and the slab of stone was placed over the top of it. There were a few chinks be-tween the stones round the top of the tomb through which a little air came, and the King had told the guards to give Polyidus a lamp and a good supply of oil; but there was no chance of escape. For not only was the entrance guarded, but the tomb was shaped like a bee-hive and the entrance was in the centre of the dome so that even if there had been no stone slab over it Polyidus could not have climbed up to it.

He sat down beside the body of the little prince, and gave way to despair. Hour after hour he sat there until he fell into a sort of coma as he waited for his long, cruel death by thirst and starvation.

Presently he was aroused by a curious rustling sound and sitting up he saw a snake gliding across the floor. As if by instinct he snatched up a stone and flung it at the snake with such good aim that in a few minutes it lay dead.

More time passed in the silence of the tomb, and then Polyidus heard another rustling, and a second snake appeared through a hole in the wall.

This time Polyidus remained quite still, for he thought: 'If the snake comes and stings me, I can only die – and such a death will be quicker and easier than that to which Minos has doomed me.'

But the snake paid no attention to him. Instead it wriggled across to its dead companion, examined the body carefully, and then glided away. Presently it returned carrying a pale-coloured herb in its mouth, which it placed on the lips of the dead serpent and then seemed to wait.

Very slowly life came back into the dead snake. First the tail moved, and then the body, and at last it turned, shook off the herb and went wriggling away into the hole in the wall with its companion, as fully alive as when it had first come into the tomb.

A thrill of hope shot through Polyidus. He rose slowly from where he sat, took up the magic herb, and placed it upon the dead lips of Glaucus. Then he waited eagerly to see what would happen. Sure enough, the prince began to breathe gently, and before long he woke up, stretched and sat up on the stone slab where he had been placed just as if he had only been asleep.

Overjoyed at this miraculous cure – and at his escape from a lingering death – Polyidus began to shout to the guards to let him out of the tomb. At first they paid no attention, thinking that he was merely begging for mercy; but when Glaucus joined in, they recognized his voice and sent in haste for Minos.

As soon as the King arrived the stone was taken off the top of the tomb and, when he had satisfied himself that his son was indeed alive and well, a rope was let down up which first Glaucus and then Polyidus climbed back into the world of life.

There was great rejoicing when the young prince was restored and King Minos heaped rewards on Polyidus, and Queen Pasiphae loaded him with jewels and gold as well.

'I thank you both,' said Polyidus, 'but I desire one thing more than any treasure, and that is to return to my own home in Greece.'

But this Minos would not allow, for he said: 'We cannot let so much wisdom and magic go out of our island. You must teach all that you know to my son Prince Glaucus whose life you have just saved – and only when he knows as much as you do will I let you leave my land.'

Very soon Polyidus discovered that there was no chance of escape from Knossos, nor any hope of leaving Crete until Minos let him go. So perforce he set himself to bring up Glaucus as master of magic arts and hidden spells. And he succeeded so well that in a few years the young man outrivalled any magician in the whole island and knew everything that his teacher could impart to him.

When he was quite sure that Glaucus could learn nothing else from Polyidus, Minos at last consented to let him leave Knossos. He ordered out a great ship in the port at Amnisos, loaded it with gold, and went to the harbour with all his court to set Polyidus on his way.

The wind was blowing strongly for Greece when the last farewells had been said, and Minos with all his followers had already left the ship, when Polyidus turned suddenly to Glaucus, who was the last to leave.

'My beloved pupil,' he said, 'there is one piece of magic which I have treasured till the last, to be a leavetaking gift for you. Do as I instruct you, and my last crumb of wisdom will be yours. Kiss me goodbye now, and as you do spit in my mouth. Then shut yours, go on shore, and do not speak a word to anyone until my ship is out of sight.'

Prince Glaucus did as the wise magician told him, and the

ship sailed away taking Polyidus and his treasure safely across the sea to a happy old age in his home at Corinth.

But when the ship had gone and Glaucus opened his mouth to explain his strange silence, he found out what the last of his master's magic spells had been – for from that moment he had forgotten everything that Polyidus had taught him.

The Sorcerer's Apprentice

In search of wonders, Eucrates the Greek sailed up the Nile to Egyptian Thebes to see the famous statue of Memnon (Pharaoh Amenophis III). This colossal carving of stone and marble sang mysteriously every morning when the rising sun shone on it, and to Eucrates the song seemed to have words of prophecy, telling him that he was himself destined to be a master of magic.

So struck by the wonder was Eucrates that he determined to remain in Egypt, the land of magic, and there learn to be a sorcerer himself.

When he consulted the learned men of Thebes they smiled, and said: 'We could indeed teach you some of our art – though most of it comes only to those who have served the gods of Egypt for many long years, and studied the spells and Words of Power left us by Thoth and Amenhotep. But for such as you, the best instructor is Pancrates the Magician of Memphis.'

And when Eucrates inquired further about this wonderful teacher he was told that Pancrates could talk to the crocodiles and ride safely on their backs through the Nile waters; and that he had lived in the tombs for three and twenty years learning all the secrets of the dead.

'How shall I know him? And where shall I find him?' asked Eucrates.

'He is even now at Thebes,' he was told. 'You will find him dressed in white linen, clean shaven, always deep in thought, able to speak Greek, but very badly. He is tall, flat-nosed, with big lips and thinnish legs.'

Furnished with this description Eucrates scoured eagerly through both Western and Eastern Thebes, and in the part that is now called Luxor he found Pancrates standing in the great courtyard of the Temple of Isis, leaning on his staff deep in contemplation.

When at last he came out of his reverie, Eucrates bowed before him and said:

'Master, I am told that you are the greatest of all the Magicians of Egypt now living, and as great as any since the far distant days of Teta and Se-Osiris. Therefore I, who have come all the way from Greece to see wonders and learn wisdom, beg you to take me as your pupil and teach me your arts – for which I will pay you well.'

At first Pancrates seemed unwilling to take on this eager young apprentice, but at length he was persuaded, and presently master and pupil embarked together on the boat which was sailing down the Nile to Memphis.

Eucrates began to learn magic on the voyage, though most of the time he was so overcome by his master's powers that he could do little himself. But in Memphis he soon began to imbibe the easier forms of magic, and before long Pancrates suggested another voyage up the Nile.

'When first we met,' he said, 'I knew nothing about you and could not trust you with the more secret spells and words of power. But now things are different, and I can safely lead you into the secret places beneath the Temple of Thoth and among the graves in the Valley of Kings at Thebes. And when you have mastered them, I will take you still further south to read the secrets that are written on the walls at Abydos and Edfu. But we must go alone and in simple guise. Therefore dismiss all your servants and be ready to set out tomorrow clad after the fashion of a scribe of the college of Amen-Ra.'

Eucrates, who loved his comforts, was not well pleased at the idea of journeying up the Nile for many weeks quite unattended. But Pancrates smiled and said:

'Surely you know by now of my magic powers sufficiently

to trust me? Although alone we shall be better attended than if we went in Pharaoh's Royal Barge!'

Accordingly they set out alone together. And Eucrates soon discovered that Pancrates had spoken nothing but the truth.

For each evening when the boat put in to shore Pancrates would enter the house where they were to lodge, take possession of their rooms, and then proceed to supply them with all they needed by means of a spell which filled Eucrates at first with amazement and then with envy.

For Pancrates would take the wooden bar from the door, or the broom-handle, or even a big wooden pestle, drape a cloak over it, and speak certain words of power. And at once it would walk and talk, and appear to everyone else to be an ordinary man. And this magical servant would go off at top speed to draw water, buy provisions and cook the evening meal. And when this was ready it would wait on them better than any servant Eucrates had ever known. And finally, when its services were completed Pancrates would speak another spell – and immediately it would fall to the ground a wooden bar, or broom-handle, or pestle, wrapped in a cloak, and nothing more.

Naturally Eucrates was eager to learn the spells and words of power which would make and unmake so excellent a serving man. But these Pancrates would not teach him, being jealous of sharing so great a secret and giving his pupil powers equal to his own.

Eucrates became more and more determined to learn the secret spell and, as Pancrates refused more and more firmly to share it with him, he at last decided to discover it without his master's knowledge.

So one evening he hid in a dark corner and was able to overhear the three words which made up the spell and remain undiscovered while Pancrates dressed up the pestle, turned it into a living creature, gave it his orders and went out for a walk.

Next morning, while Pancrates was transacting some business with the Priests of Hathor at Denderah, where they were staying for a few days, Eucrates decided that the moment had come to see whether the spell would work for him as well as it did when Pancrates spoke it. So he took the pestle, wrapped it in a cloak, and pronounced the words of power in a low, solemn voice.

At once the pestle rose up and came to life, saying: 'Master, what shall I do?'

'Go to the well in the courtyard and fetch me water!' commanded Eucrates, 'And pour the water into my bath!'

The pestle snatched up a bucket, sped out into the yard, and returned a moment later with it full of water which it poured into the bath. Then it sped out and back again with the bucket refilled, and continued to do so at lightning speed.

Very soon the bath was overflowing, and Eucrates exclaimed: 'Stop! Stop! That is enough!' But the pestle paid no attention. It dashed in and out with the buckets of water; and very soon the floor was inches deep in it and the flood was rising round Eucrates's ankles.

In vain the magician's apprentice shouted and stormed, muttered words of power and chanted spells. The pestle-servant did not stop for an instant.

Now Eucrates grew afraid that Pancrates would return and be angry. So in desperation he snatched up an axe and split the wooden pestle at a blow.

But to his horror and amazement the two halves each rose up immediately, each seized a bucket, and each continued pouring water into the bath, while the flood rose higher and higher in the house.

Suddenly Pancrates appeared at the door. He took one look, saw what had happened, and glared furiously at Eucrates – who sprang quickly out of the house, fearing some punishment.

A few moments later he returned cautiously to find the two halves of the split pestle lying on the floor, two harmless and useless pieces of wood.

But of Pancrates there was no sign. And though he sought for him up and down the Nile for many months, Eucrates never saw him again.

And although he knew the spell for turning a piece of wood into a servant, Eucrates never again dared to speak it. For he did not know the spell for turning the servant back into a piece of wood – and he was afraid of starting another flood that might this time engulf the whole world since only the sorcerer would know how to stop it, and his apprentice did not.

Virgilius the Sorcerer

IN the days of Ancient Rome there lived a boy called Virgilius who, from an early age, decided to become a Magician. He was able to do this on account of an extraordinary chance which befell him when he was a young student at Tolenten.

Like any other schoolboy, Virgilius enjoyed a half-holiday, and on one particular occasion, as soon as the schoolmaster had dismissed the class, he set out as fast as he could walk to the near-by mountains.

Wandering in deep valleys and along high shelves of rock he came to a cave which offered good scope for exploration. Virgilius was a bold boy, and he plunged into the cave without a thought of the dangers that might be in wait for him there.

The cave was narrow at first, but soon opened out into a wide cavern. He had groped his way through darkness in the narrow portion; but in the wide cavern a little light came filtering down through a hole high above him that was shaded over with tall grasses and bushes.

As he paused under this hole, he heard a voice calling him very softly: 'Virgilius! Virgilius!' He looked about him, but could see no one either in the cave or among the vegetation round the hole in the roof.

'Who calls me?' he shouted. 'And where are you?'

'Virgilius!' came the voice, 'Look on the ground before where you stand, and you will see a round disc of stone held in place by a bolt.'

'I see it,' answered Virgilius.

'Then,' said the voice, 'draw back the bolt and set me free.'

'Who are you that speaks to me from beneath the floor of this cave?' asked Virgilius.

'I am a spirit, shut up here till Doomsday,' answered the voice. 'Only a mortal man can free me – and if you are he, I will give you Magic Books that will make you the greatest Magician who has ever lived.'

'Give me the books first,' said Virgilius, for he already suspected that the spirit with whom he had to deal was an evil one, imprisoned for terrible crimes.

Since there was no help for it, the Evil Spirit told him where the books were hidden on a shelf high up in the side of the cave, and when he had taken them down and glanced into them, Virgilius drew back the bolt.

At once the round stone sprang open on its hinge, and out of the small round hole so revealed there crawled and scrambled and wriggled a terrible black fiend three times the size of a man.

'Oh Master, Master!' cried Virgilius flinging himself to the floor and knocking his forehead upon the ground as if in homage to a superior being. 'Oh, Master, Master! How could you delude a poor boy so? I thought that you came out of that small hole in the floor; but one so great could never pass through so tiny a space.'

'Do you doubt my powers – or my sufferings?' cried the Evil Spirit. 'Watch, and I will prove both to you in a single action!'

So saying the Evil Spirit wriggled and scrambled and crawled back through the small round hole in the stone floor. The moment it had done so, Virgilius clapped the round stone disc back into place and shot the bolt, crying:

'For your evil deeds you have been imprisoned beneath this stone until Doomsday! Until Doomsday remain imprisoned there!'

So saying, Virgilius picked up the pile of Magic Books and returned at full speed to Tolenten.

There for the next ten years he studied the Magic Books,

and by the end of that time had mastered every spell and charm in them and had become the most learned and powerful Magician of the day.

At the end of this time his mother sent to Virgilius begging him to return to Rome as she was growing old and ill, and was being robbed of her rightful income by all her late husband's rich relatives.

Virgilius returned and was received honourably, for the accounts of his great learning and knowledge of Magic had preceded him. But when he demanded the return of the last ten years' income which had been stolen from his mother, the Emperor (who had received a half share of all the spoils) said oftily that he would give Virgilius his answer in four years' time when he had weighed all the evidence.

Virgilius said nothing. But when harvest time came he hid away all his corn so cleverly that even the tax-collectors could not find a single grain of it. And when the fruit was ripe, he hid it all by enchantment. And the same with the wine, after the vintage, so that not one drop came to the Emperor nor any of his friends who had hitherto robbed the mother of Virgilius of nearly all her due.

This angered his enemies so much that they set out with an army and surrounded the castle where Virgilius and his mother lived. But Virgilius cast a spell on them of such strength that they were frozen where they stood and remained fixed for a day and a night. And when he released them, they slunk back to Rome with no fight left in them.

But before they went Virgilius sent a message to the Emperor by them: 'My lord Emperor, I will wait the four years you decree for my judgement – but I'll take all my due during that time, and care not what you may do or try to do to prevent me.'

The Emperor was not accustomed to being thwarted in this

way, and he immediately set out for the castle with a large regiment of soldiers. But when they drew near, Virgilius by means of his magic arts surrounded the castle with a deep, ice-cold river; and he surrounded the Emperor's army with just such another river, so that they were caught between the two and could move neither forward nor back.

They had few provisions with them, and very soon they were starving – a state which Virgilius made all the worse for them by causing his cooks to prepare savoury meals and roast great joints of meat just on his side of the inner river.

The Emperor was in despair; but he would not pardon Virgilius. He and his army would surely have starved, had it not chanced that another magician happened to be between the magic rivers. By his arts he was able to dry up that nearest to the castle, and cast a great drowsiness on Virgilius and all his followers.

'Now we have him!' cried the Emperor, and attacked promptly with all his forces.

Keeping himself awake with the utmost difficulty, Virgilius made his way to his study and opened one of the Magic Books he had obtained from the Evil Spirit in the cave. Very soon he found the spell he wanted, repeated it and uttered a great Word of Power.

The very castle shook at the sound. But the Emperor and all his men were at once held fast as if turned to stone – some climbing up scaling ladders, others with arrows half drawn at their bow-strings. This new charm also put an end to that of the Emperor's magician, so that Virgilius and his men were able to shake off their drowsiness or wake from the sleep into which many of them had already fallen.

Virgilius left all his victims exactly as they were for another day. Then he disenchanted the Emperor and caused him to be brought before him. And the Emperor was so thoroughly frightened by now that he agreed at once not only to restore to Virgilius all that had been stolen from him, but to make him Court Magician immediately.

Thereupon Virgilius revoked both the spell which had made the river and that which had turned all his attackers into stone. Then he feasted them all handsomely in his castle, and sent them back to Rome, bestowing a gift on each.

He himself followed later with the Emperor. And as proof of his loyalty he raised a square tower for him the very next day on the highest hill in Rome. This was a magic tower, and if the Emperor stood in any corner of it he could hear every word that was being spoken in that quarter of Rome – and so it became impossible for any plots to be made against him.

In spite of all his wisdom and his knowledge of magical arts, Virgilius was not always successful in his ventures. His very next made him, for a time, the laughing stock of Rome. This chanced when he fell in love with the noble Lady Febilla who dwelt in a high tower in the middle of the city. He was able by his arts to tell her of his love without visiting her, and she was able to send back a message. This was to bid him visit her on a dark night, when she would let down a basket from her window in the top of the tower in which he might be pulled up to her room.

Virgilius, full of delight, got into the basket and was pulled up – but only half-way. Febilla was determined to mock him, and show him that he could not get all that he wanted, Magician though he was: for she did not love him in the least – indeed she rather despised him. So she left him hanging in the basket half-way up the tower; and when the sun rose and the people of Rome came into the market place beneath, Febilla pointed Virgilius out to them, saying:

'This rogue of a Magician tried to carry me off in the middle of the night. But look at him now!'

And all the people looked, and laughed, and made fun of Virgilius – the magician who had been outwitted by a woman – until he was nearly mad with rage and shame.

At length the Emperor heard what had happened and commanded that Virgilius should be set free at once.

As soon as the Magician was out of the basket he dashed home to his castle, vowing vengeance. And very soon he hit upon a plan which his magic powers made possible.

Quite suddenly next day all the fires in Rome went out, and the people discovered that by no possible means could they strike a light. Very soon angry and frightened crowds began to gather in the streets and advance towards the Emperor's Palace, shouting that the city was bewitched.

Naturally the Emperor turned to Virgilius for advice, and the Magician replied with a cold smile:

'Bring the Lady Febilla to the rostrum in the Forum wearing a single garment of white, and chain her there by the ankle. As soon as night falls, this white garment will burst into flames and go on burning all night, without harming her in the least. Only by noon tomorrow will the white garment be completely consumed – and only then must you set Febilla free and allow her to return home. Meanwhile, from sunset tonight until noon tomorrow let everyone in Rome come to the Forum and light a torch or a lamp from Febilla's burning robe and carry it home to their hearths. Each must come separately, for they will not be able to light anything but the fire on their own hearths with the magic flame.'

As there was no help for it, the Emperor commanded Febilla to be chained on the stone rostrum in the Forum wearing only a thin white dress. And, as Virgilius had predicted, as soon as the sun set this dress turned into white flame which did no harm to Febilla but at which every Roman in the city was able to light a lamp or torch.

By noon next day all the fires were re-lighted. And as soon

as the sun reached the zenith, Febilla's dress fell from her in ashes and the magic fire died out from about her.

After this the Emperor was minded to slay Virgilius for playing such a trick and putting a noble lady of Rome to such shame. But Virgilius departed from Rome by his magic, and built himself a castle on the edge of the sea where the city of Naples still stands.

That castle was itself the work of magic, for its foundations were laid on eggs – and yet that castle stands to this day, and is still known as the Castell dell'Ovo – 'the Castle of the Egg'. Nor was the Emperor able to take it or seize Virgilius: for when he sent an army to besiege it, the Magician turned all the springs of fresh water salt whenever a Roman tried to drink from them or draw water; and even when it rained all the water the Roman army was able to catch became salty as soon as they tried to drink it.

So the army turned back, and the Emperor gave up any idea of trying to imprison or punish Virgilius. And in time he forgave him, and made him his chief Magician once more.

Before this happened, however, Virgilius had accomplished the most extraordinary exploit of his whole career, and won a Princess to be his wife.

By his magic arts he discovered that the daughter of the Sultan of Babylon was the most beautiful Princess in the world; so he set to work and constructed a kind of magic bridge through the air all the way from Italy to Babylon over which he passed straight from his castle into her own private apartments of the Sultan's Palace.

Virgilius fell in love with the Princess on sight, and, what is more, she fell in love with him and was quite ready to visit him in his own home. So he took her in his arms and carried her swiftly over the magic bridge to his orchard in his castle; and there she remained happily with him for many days. And when he had shown her all his treasures, and the guards made of metal who protected his castle from any attack, and all the other wonders of his castle, she was all the more willing to stay.

But at length she felt that she must return home for a while, for she knew that her father the Sultan would be wondering about her mysterious disappearance. And indeed the whole city of Babylon had been in a turmoil, with great rewards offered for anyone who could find the missing Princess. But the Sultan was not anxious to give any reward to anyone when, one morning, the serving women sent to tell him that they had found the Princess sleeping peacefully on her bed.

He hastened to her room, however, and when she woke he asked her where she had been and how she had returned so mysteriously.

'Father,' she answered, 'I dreamed that a handsome man from some strange land came to visit me. And presently he took me through the air over land and sea to his castle and his orchard. All the time I have been away I have dwelt in perfect happiness with him, and seen no other living soul but him alone.'

Then the Sultan pretended to be interested only in discovering where the Princess's midnight visitor came from, and to what land he took her.

'For you have been away many days, and therefore it is no dream, but art magic,' he told her.

So the Princess agreed to give Virgilius a glass of special wine which would cast him into a deep sleep, and then tell her father so that he could be present when Virgilius woke, and question him.

But when Virgilius came and, suspecting nothing, drank of the drugged wine and fell instantly asleep, the Sultan caused him to be bound in chains and cast into a deep dungeon.

Next day Virgilius was drawn out of the dungeon and brought before the Sultan and all the court.

'You are welcome, stranger,' said the Sultan grimly. 'In exchange for the pleasures you have enjoyed in your own land, you shall suffer a cruel and shameful death in mine for the dishonour you have brought upon my daughter.'

'If I carried her away, I have also brought her back, when I might have kept her for ever in my castle,' said Virgilius. 'However, I promise solemnly that if you let me return to my own land I will never come to Babylon again.'

'That shall avail you nothing!' cried the Sultan, perhaps suspecting that Virgilius might be able to convey the Princess to his castle without coming for her in person. 'You have brought dishonour upon her, and here and now you shall die the death you deserve.'

'If you put him to death, I will die with him!' cried the Princess.

'That I had already decided,' answered the Sultan. 'You shall indeed suffer the price of your shame. Together you shall be burned to death this very day in the great square before all the people of Babylon.'

So they were led down through the city to the great square where two stakes were set up to which they were to be fastened.

But the moment Virgilius was freed from his fetters to be led forward and bound to the stake, he raised his arms suddenly and cried aloud a great Word of Power. At it everyone fell silent and drew away in fear – except the Princess who sprang to his side.

Then Virgilius cast a spell over all the people in Babylon so that they believed everyone of them that the great river Euphrates which flows near-by had risen suddenly and flooded the whole city. Everyone, from the Sultan downwards, thought no more of anything but escaping from the rising waters, and on every side they struck out desperately – swimming their hardest to escape from the imaginary flood.

As soon as he and the Princess were left alone, Virgilius conjured up his bridge of air and passed over it with her. Then, directly they reached his castle in Naples he waved his hands and the bridge was no more. Nor was the Princess ever seen again in Babylon.

But she and Virgilius lived long and happily together in the Castle of the Egg; and the Emperor forgave the great Magician for defying him. In return Virgilius did many Works of Magic for the protection of Rome, and was ever afterwards remembered as the greatest Magician who had ever lived in the land of Italy.

PART TWO

Magicians of the Middle Ages

Aladdin and the African Magician

WHEN the Arabs ruled more than half of the known world, from Morocco in North Africa to beyond India and even to China, and Haroun-al-Raschid was Caliph in Baghdad, the capital of this mighty empire, there lived a magician in Africa who was altogether wicked – as were most magicians among the Arabs.

Like the rest of the Eastern Magicians, the African Magician drew most of his magic from the use of talismans and charms which were able to summon up mighty spirits, or Jinn, whose amazing powers were perforce at the service of those who knew how to use and command them.

After forty years of study in the black art the African Magician discovered that the most powerful talisman in the whole world was an old copper lamp which was hidden in an underground garden near a certain city of China. From some of the lesser Jinn whom he was able to summon with the aid of talismans already in his own possession, the African Magician discovered exactly how he would be able to obtain possession of the Lamp; and armed with this knowledge he set out for China.

When he reached the city nearest to the hiding place of the Lamp he set about seeking for some boy whom he could use for his schemes – and who would not be missed if he disappeared. Very soon he discovered just the boy he wanted, the only son of the widow of a tailor called Mustapha, a boy who would do no work but spent his time playing in the streets with other waifs and strays even more disreputable than himself.

Next day, accordingly, the African Magician stopped this boy, whose name was Aladdin, and said to him:

'Are you by any chance the son of Mustapha the tailor?'

'I am,' answered Aladdin in surprise. 'But my father has been dead for many years.'

'I knew I could not be mistaken!' cried the African Magician. 'Mustapha looked just as you do when I last saw him many years ago when, like you, he was but fifteen. Oh my beloved nephew, I am your uncle, your long lost uncle!'

With that he flung his arms round Aladdin and kissed him and wept over him, saying: 'I have been many years on my journey to visit my beloved younger brother Mustapha. Although he is dead, he lives again in you, who are his very image as he was when I bade farewell to him forty years ago and went forth to seek my fortune. My fortune is made, and I came to share it with Mustapha. He is dead – but now I shall share it with you.'

Aladdin was delighted with this news, and even more so when the African Magician drew out a bag of money and handed it to him, saying:

'Take this to your mother, and tell her that I shall visit you both for dinner tomorrow.'

'Yes,' said Aladdin's mother when he had dashed home with his wonderful news. 'Your father had a brother. But he always said that he had died many years ago – and I certainly never saw him.'

But she joined Aladdin in rejoicing over their good fortune, and had a fine dinner waiting for the African Magician when he arrived next day laden with presents for them.

After this the false uncle took charge of Aladdin, bought him fine clothes, and talked of setting him up in business with a well-stocked shop of his own.

'But there is no hurry,' he said. 'I have enough for us all. Enjoy yourself for a few days. And to begin with, come walking with me through the fashionable parts of the town, and into the fine gardens on the outskirts.'

Aladdin was delighted with all this, and set off gaily with the African Magician to flaunt his new clothes. After they had walked through the squares and bazaars of the town, the false uncle led him through the gardens, and then out into the country and away towards the hills.

Presently Aladdin began to get tired, for he was a lazy boy who was not used to taking much exercise.

'Uncle,' he said, 'we've gone far beyond the gardens, and I can see nothing before me but hills and desert. And if we go much further I don't think I'll be strong enough to walk all the way back to the city.'

'Take courage, dear nephew,' answered the Magician, 'we have not much further to go, and I want to show you the most wonderful garden of all.'

So they went on, the Magician telling stories to keep Aladdin's mind occupied, until they came to a narrow valley in the hills, which he knew by magic arts to be the place he had come all the way from Africa to find.

'We need go no further now,' said the Magician. 'This is where the entrance to the garden lies hidden. Do as I tell you, and you will see wonders such as no one ever saw before, and return home richly rewarded. To begin with, collect a good pile of sticks while I kindle a fire.'

Aladdin had no difficulty in doing this, for the place was littered with dead branches. When he had collected a large pile he found that the Magician had struck fire with his flint and steel, and they soon had a merry blaze going.

Then, uttering mystic words, the Magician threw a magic powder on to the flames and a dense cloud of smoke arose. He spoke a deep-sounding charm, and the earth shook and opened before them revealing a square stone in a little hollow. The stone was about eighteen inches each way, and in its centre was a copper ring.

Aladdin turned to run with a cry of fear, but the Magician

caught hold of him by the back of the neck and shook him:

'There's nothing to be afraid of, you young fool! Keep still, or you'll ruin everything!' he shouted. And then, mastering his violent temper with difficulty, he went on: 'Dearest nephew, this is the moment at which you must show by your courage and obedience that you are indeed worthy of the great future I plan for you. Let me explain: Under this stone is hidden a treasure which will make you the richest man in the world – and only you can touch it in safety and bring it out into the light of day.'

'But, uncle, I am not strong enough to pull up this stone,' said Aladdin, much impressed. 'Will you help me?'

'That cannot be,' answered the Magician. 'If I touch anything in this enchanted place, it will become mine – but if you pull up the stone and do all that I tell you, the treasure shall be yours, and no one will be able to take it from you. As for the stone, all you have to do is to seize hold of the ring and as you pull cry aloud the names of your father and your grandfather. When the stone is raised, you will find beneath it a narrow stair leading to a door, which will open as you reach it. Beyond that are more stairs leading into three halls, one beyond the other. In each hall you will pass great bronze tubs filled to the top with objects of gold and silver. But do not touch any of them even with the edge of your sleeves – or some terrible fate will befall you. Pass through the three halls and out into the garden beyond, which is planted with beautiful trees – from which you may pluck and keep as many of the fruits which hang on them as you can carry: you will find them a treasure indeed. And, to reward me for having shown you how to make your fortune, and not having taken all for myself as I could so easily have done, go to the end of the garden and climb the fifty steps to the terrace. On it you will find a niche in which an old copper lamp is burning. Extinguish it and empty out the liquid within it: it is not oil, and the lamp will dry directly, and will not even be warm. So put it carefully in your robe and bring it back for me as a memento of this day of days.'

All fell out as the Magician had said. Aladdin had no difficulty in raising the stone as soon as he had spoken the names of his father and grandfather; the door at the foot of the stairs which were then revealed opened as he reached it. He passed through the three halls and was able to resist the temptation to help himself to the gold and silver objects in the bronze tubs. Beyond he found a strange, shadowy garden of trees on which shimmered fruits of red and green and blue, violet and yellow and white – and of these he picked as many as he could carry in his wide sleeves and loose robe, not know-ing that they were precious jewels: rubies and emeralds and turquoises, amethysts and sapphires and diamonds. He found the old copper lamp burning dimly in the niche at the top of the fifty steps, extinguished and emptied it and pushed it away into the front of his robe among the great weight of gems. Then he returned slowly by the way he had come, and reached the steps beyond the door – which closed behind him the moment he had passed through it. These steps were very steep and narrow, and Aladdin paused halfway up them to rest – too exhausted to go further.

'Give me your hand, uncle, and pull me up!' cried Aladdin. 'I'm too tired to go further.'

'Pass the lamp first,' said the Magician. 'It is probably that which is encumbering you, and making it so difficult for you to climb out.'

'No, it's not that,' answered Aladdin, 'that's no trouble at all. I can carry that quite easily, and so I've decided to keep it.'

By this Aladdin merely meant that if he had to leave behind some of the jewelled fruits because they were too heavy to bring up the steps with him, he wouldn't leave the lamp. But the Magician, whose temper was short at any time, and who was so anxious about the success of his schemes that he was ready to suspect anything, thought immediately that Aladdin had learned something special about the lamp and was trying to keep it for himself, flew into a violent rage, and cried: 'Give me the lamp at once, or it will be the worse for you!'

'It won't do me any harm,' answered Aladdin. 'So please help me out of here, and believe that I know what is best for me.'

This so confirmed the Magician's false suspicions, that with a yell of fury he flung the last handful of magic powder into the fire and cried aloud the Word of Power. At once the square stone slid back into place and the earth closed over it with a low roar of thunder.

Then, when it was too late, the Magician realized that he had thrown away his chance of gaining the lamp, for never again could he cause the ground to open and the stone to slip aside.

So with many bitter curses, he set out for his home in Africa, without sparing a single thought, save those of hatred and condemnation, for poor Aladdin abandoned to his fate in the enchanted cave.

And in the enchanted cave Aladdin might have sat until he died of hunger and thirst, had it not been for a further over-sight on the part of the African Magician. For he had given Aladdin a ring to wear which was to guard him from harm while he was under the ground – and this he had left with him when he shut him in and left him to die.

Aladdin also had forgotten about the ring, or considered it of no importance. But on the second day of his captivity, having given up all hope of life, he was clasping his hands in prayer – when he happened to rub the ring.

At once a Jinnee of enormous size and a most horrid countenance rose out of the ground before him, so tall that he touched the vaulted roof of the underground hall.

'What is your command, Oh Lord of the Ring?' cried the Jinnee. 'I am ready to obey you as your slave – I, and the other Slaves of the Ring.'

At any other time Aladdin would have fainted with terror at this horrible apparition. But he was already so numbed with fear and despair that he hardly seemed to notice. There was only one idea in his mind, and this he voiced in a cry of entreaty:

'Take me out of this terrible place!'

Scarcely had he spoken when the earth opened above him and the floor seemed to rise beneath him. In another moment he was lying in the little valley by the ashes of the fire, with the sun shining in his face so brightly that it took him a little while to see where he was after his two days in the dimness of the underground hall.

As soon as he had recovered a bit, Aladdin made his way back to the city and told his mother about his extraordinary adventures.

'I doubted very much if that man could be my husband's brother,' she said shaking her head. 'It seems that he was a magician – and wicked, like most of those who practise his black arts.'

'Never mind about him now,' said Aladdin. 'What I want is a good big meal, as I've had nothing to eat for over two days.'

'Alas!' cried his mother, 'there is no food left in the house, and no money to buy it with.'

'I think we can remedy that,' said Aladdin. 'Here is the old brass lamp which the Magician wanted me to fetch out of the underground garden. It ought to sell for quite a good sum of money.'

'It's very dirty,' said his mother. 'I'll clean it up a bit before you take it.' She began to polish it with her apron. But scarcely had she rubbed it once when instantly a hideous and

gigantic Jinnee rose out of the ground before her and cried with a voice as loud as thunder:

'What are thy commands? I am ready to obey thee as thy slave – the slave of whoever holds the Lamp, both I and the other Slaves of the Lamp!'

Aladdin's mother was too terrified to do anything but fall back on the ottoman and cover her face. But Aladdin, who had already had some experience of Jinn, when the Slave of the Ring appeared to him in the cave, snatched up the Lamp and exclaimed:

'I am hungry! Slave of the Lamp, bring us food!'

The Jinnee disappeared and returned a moment later carrying a splendid banquet on golden dishes. These he placed on the table, adding bottles of wine and silver goblets to complete the meal, bowed low before Aladdin – and vanished.

From this day began Aladdin's good fortune. With the aid of the Magic Lamp he could obtain all that he wanted – though for several years he was content with keeping his mother and himself in food and drink, fine clothes and a comfortable house. He also gave up his idle games with his former companions of the streets and began to spend his time in the company of students and merchants and other even more important people who readily allowed this richly dressed young man to learn from their discourses about all those things in which each of them was expert.

One day when Aladdin had grown into a handsome young man it chanced that the Sultan's daughter, the Princess Badroulboudour, was to pass through the streets on her way to the bath. The Sultan's orders were that everyone was to remain in their houses and keep their doors and shutters closed – in spite of the fact that the Princess, like all other women in that country, would be wearing a veil – and that she would be carried in a litter with closed curtains.

In a sudden fit of curiosity Aladdin hid himself carefully

near the entrance to the bath, and was able to see the Princess quite unveiled and close at hand. Badroulboudour was the loveliest Princess in all the world – and Aladdin fell in love with her at sight.

With great difficulty he persuaded his mother to go to the Sultan and ask the Princess's hand in marriage for her son. When at last she consented, it took many days before the Sultan was prepared even to receive her and listen to her request.

When at last she knelt before him and asked him to give his daughter in marriage to Aladdin, all the great lords and viziers expected the Sultan to order her and her audacious son to instant execution. But it so happened that the Sultan was in a good mood that day, and said with a smile:

'It is usual when royal wooers send to ask the hand of a Princess in marriage for them to bring some small present to her father to show both the depth of their love – and of their purses. What do you bring me wrapped up in that cloth?'

For answer Aladdin's mother untied the bundle which she was carrying and laid before him all the jewels which Aladdin had plucked from the magic fruit trees in the underground garden of the Lamp.

The Sultan and his court gazed on them – and cried out in amazement: for never before had they seen such a treasure of large and perfect jewels.

'It seems to me', said the Sultan at length, 'that if Aladdin can send such a present as this, he will be able to bestow on his bride treasures beyond all imagining. And so it seems to me that Aladdin should marry the Princess Badroulboudour.'

This displeased the Grand Vizier very much: for the Sultan had been considering his son as the best possible husband for the Princess.

'I think, most noble Sultan,' he said quickly, 'that you

should wait three months before bestowing your daughter's hand on this unknown Aladdin. Let us see at least how constant he will prove in his affections.'

This seemed wise advice, and the Sultan said to Aladdin's mother:

'Go home to your son and tell him that if he sends you again in three months' time with the same request, I am minded to grant it.'

Aladdin was delighted when he heard this news. It was all he could do to wait in patience until the time was up, and he could not help counting the weeks and the days and even the hours until the Princess should be his.

But one day, after two months were passed, Aladdin's mother happened to go out for a walk into the city and found the streets decorated and the people out in their best clothes.

'What is happening?' she inquired.

'Where do you come from that you ask such a question!' they said. 'Do you not know that this very day the Princess Badroulboudour, our Sultan's only daughter, is being married to the son of the Grand Vizier?'

When she heard this, Aladdin's mother hurried home as fast as she could:

'All is lost, my son!' she gasped. 'The Sultan has broken his promise, and the Princess is being married this very day to the Grand Vizier's son.'

Aladdin was as one thunderstruck. But in a few minutes his mind cleared and he saw what to do. 'There is no need to worry, mother,' he said quietly. 'This bridegroom shall be the unhappiest man in the world tonight, and each night until he gives up the Princess!'

So saying, he went into his own room, took the Magic Lamp down from the shelf and rubbed it. When the Jinnee appeared with his usual 'What are thy commands? I am ready to obey thee as thy slave, and the slave of those who have the

Lamp in their hands, both I and the other Slaves of the Lamp,'
Aladdin gave him his orders and bade him go about them
swiftly.

The result was that the moment the Princess and the Grand
Vizier's son were left alone together, the Slave of the Lamp
carried the bed with them on it to Aladdin's house in one
moment. Then he took the unlucky bridegroom and left him
in an outhouse, breathed upon him so that he could not move
– and next morning he was almost frozen to death when the
Jinnee carried him and the Princess back to the Palace just
before the Sultan and Sultana came to visit their daughter and
son-in-law.

This happened several nights running, until at length the
wretched bridegroom could stand it no longer – and at his
request, as well as that of the Princess, the marriage was
declared null and void.

Not long after this the three months were up, and Aladdin's
mother presented herself once more before the Sultan to ask
for the fulfilment of his promise to bestow his daughter upon
Aladdin.

The Sultan had hoped and expected to see no more of her
and hear no more of Aladdin's pretensions to be his son-in-
law. Now he took counsel with his Grand Vizier and soon hit
upon a scheme which he felt sure would put an end to Aladdin's suit.

'I am ready and willing to fulfil my promise and give my
daughter in marriage to your son,' he said. 'But of course I
must receive such a bridal gift that I may be in no doubt of
this Aladdin's wealth – of his ability to keep the Princess
Badroulboudour in the state to which she had always been
accustomed. So let him send me forty large basins of solid
gold, each filled with jewels such as those you brought me
before; and let these basins be carried by forty black slaves,
each with a white slave-girl in attendance – young, beautiful

and richly dressed. As soon as I have received these, Aladdin shall marry the Princess.'

Aladdin's mother returned with this message, thinking that here was an end of her son's chances of winning the bride whom he desired. But Aladdin simply rubbed the Lamp, summoned the Jinnee who was Slave of the Lamp, and issued his commands – which were promptly obeyed so fully that the Sultan gave immediate orders for Aladdin to be brought before him so that the wedding-date could be fixed.

Aladdin promptly rubbed the Lamp once more, and when the Jinnee appeared, he said: 'Slave of the Lamp, bring me a richer and more magnificent dress than was ever worn by any monarch; a horse surpassing in beauty and excellence any in the Sultan's stables; a retinue of slaves richly clad to wait upon me; six slave-girls bearing garments of the richest silk for my mother, and ten thousand pieces of gold in each of ten separate purses.'

When all this was accomplished, Aladdin rode in state through the streets to the Palace, his servants scattering handfuls of gold among the crowds who gathered to see him pass, and was welcomed by the Sultan as if he had been the very Caliph of Baghdad himself.

The wedding was fixed for the next day, but before he left the Palace to prepare himself for it, Aladdin said to the Sultan:

'My lord and father, I wish to build a palace worthy of my bride to be. My workmen are all in readiness, and all that is needful is prepared, save only an acre of ground on which to build it.'

Then the Sultan replied, leading Aladdin to a window: 'Yonder stretch of parkland is yours: I had planned to build upon it, but had not yet found architects and masons who could prepare a building such as I desire. You, I feel certain, can accomplish it.'

'By tomorrow it will be ready to receive my bride!'

declared Aladdin, and forthwith took his leave – for, even with the Slave of the Lamp to perform all his commands he had much to do.

Next morning the Sultan looked out of his window and was dumbfounded to see a palace built of marble and gold, cedar wood and ivory, and inlaid with precious stones standing amidst the trees of the park scarcely a furlong distant from his own Royal Palace.

Aladdin's Palace, though it had grown into being overnight, seemed as if it had always stood there. In the kitchens and sculleries the cooks and scullions were busy preparing a great wedding feast; in the stables the grooms were rubbing down the horses while the stable-boys filled the mangers with fresh corn and swept the stone floors; in the gardens the gardeners were already at work – and in the apartments prepared for the bride the slave girls were preparing for their new mistress, laying out jewels and veils and rich robes, preparing rare scents and powders and cosmetics, and carrying up bowls of fruit, flasks of wine and caskets of sweetmeats.

A carpet of the finest velvet was stretched from the gate of the Sultan's Palace all the way to the bridal chamber in Aladdin's Palace, and before the setting of the sun that day Aladdin led the Princess Badroulboudour along it as his wife.

While Aladdin was winning a Princess to be his wife and becoming a Prince himself, and the richest man in all China, the African Magician had not given up all hope of obtaining the Magic Lamp.

He was so sure that Aladdin had died in the cave that for several years he spent all his time and art on discovering how to open the ground above it for a second time and regain the Lamp which had been so nearly his from among the mouldering bones of his luckless victim.

At last his spells and charms enabled him to pierce the

distance, and see distinctly into the cave with the staircase leading to the hall and the garden where jewels grew on all the trees. Sending out his spirit, like an Egyptian *Ka*, across the world, he was able to search the stairs, the hall, and every corner of the garden; but what was his amazement to discover there was no sign of Aladdin – and no Magic Lamp!

A little necromancy showed him that Aladdin was still alive, and by his knowledge of astrology he discovered that the beggar-boy had become the richest man in all China.

The moment he discovered this, the African Magician set out for the East: for he knew that only with the aid of the Magic Lamp could Aladdin have won such wealth.

In due time he arrived at the city where he had first found Aladdin playing in the streets, and soon heard all about the fabulously wealthy Prince Aladdin who had married the Sultan's only child the Princess Badroulboudour and lived in a Palace far more glorious than that of the Sultan himself.

'And when the Sultan dies,' the people told him, 'Prince Aladdin is sure to succeed him. And he'll make the best ruler this land has ever had. Why, every week, even now, he rides through the city scattering handfuls of gold coins among us!'

When he heard all this, the African Magician nearly choked with rage and jealousy. But he set himself all the more eagerly to the business of ruining Aladdin and gaining not only the Magic Lamp, but the Princess and her Palace for himself.

He very soon discovered that Aladdin had gone hunting for a week, and would still not return for several days. He also practised the magic art of geomancy to such good effect that he discovered that the Magic Lamp was still in the Palace.

Accordingly he disguised himself in old clothes, purchased several dozen new copper lamps, and set out through the streets near the Palace of Aladdin, crying: 'New lamps for old! Who'll take new lamps for old?'

His plan worked admirably. The Princess Badroulboudour was getting bored with being by herself, and when she heard her handmaidens laughing among themselves, she was only too eager to ask what had amused them.

'There's a mad merchant in the street outside,' they told her. 'He's exchanging new copper lamps for old ones. Did you ever hear of anything so ridiculous? He'll soon have a basket full of worthless old lamps instead of the beautiful new, shining copper ones which he is giving away.'

The Princess laughed. Then she exclaimed: 'Well, let us exchange an old lamp for a new one too! There's an old, tarnished lamp on the shelf in my husband's private room: go and fetch that and see if the mad merchant will give us a new one in exchange for it.'

The handmaids did as she told them, and soon brought her back a fine new lamp. But the African Magician recognized the Magic Lamp at once, and hid it quickly in his robe. Then he hastened away, still crying, 'New lamps for old! Who'll give old lamps for new ones?' until he reached the edge of the city.

Here he hid the basket of worthless lamps and set out for the near-by mountains, which he reached as the sun was setting.

As soon as it was dark he took the Magic Lamp from the breast of his robe and rubbed it eagerly. At once the Jinnee appeared and bowed low before him, saying: 'What are thy commands? I am ready to obey thee as thy slave, and the slave of any who holds the Lamp in his hands – I and the other Slaves of the Lamp.'

'I command you!' said the African Magician triumphantly, 'I command you instantly to take up Aladdin's Palace which you and the other Slaves of the Lamp have erected in this city; take it exactly as it is, with everything in it, both dead and alive, and transport it, and me also, to my home in the utmost confines of Africa.'

The Jinnee bowed; and immediately he and the other Jinn who were the Slaves of the Lamp lifted up the Palace with everything in it, and carried it and the African Magician all the way to Africa in a matter of moments so softly that no one in it felt more than a couple of tiny trembles as it was taken up and set down.

Next morning the Sultan looked out of his window, as was his custom, to admire Aladdin's Palace shining with gold and jewels and marble among the trees – and there was no Palace. He summoned his Grand Vizier in haste – and he too could see no Palace.

Then the Sultan's anger was terrible. 'Send out men and bring Aladdin bound before me!' he shouted. 'He is a wicked Magician who has cheated me by his arts and stolen away my daughter to work some hideous spell upon her!'

Rejoicing at the downfall of Aladdin, whom he had always hated, the Grand Vizier set out at the head of a troop of soldiers, met Aladdin who was on his way home from hunting, bound him and dragged him before the Sultan.

'Wretch!' cried the Sultan as soon as he saw him. 'Give me back my daughter, or you shall die instantly!' and he beckoned to the Royal Executioner who at once stepped forward and raised his mighty sword above his head.

By this time Aladdin had discovered about the disappearance of his Palace, and guessed what had happened.

'Most noble Sultan and dear father of my bride!' he exclaimed. 'Do not be hasty. What has chanced is none of my doing: there is a wicked Magician from Africa, the most evil wizard in the world, who has sworn to ruin me and make your daughter his wife. By art magic, with the aid of Jinn and Afreets, he has carried her away and with her my Palace. Give me but forty days – and if in that time the Princess Badroulboudour is not restored to you, and with her my Palace, I will give myself up readily to death.'

'Be it as you wish,' said the Sultan, who realized that the only chance of ever seeing his beloved daughter again lay in Aladdin's possible power to overcome the African Magician. 'But fail me not, or you shall die!'

Aladdin went out from the Sultan's Palace and wandered through the streets of the city. Although he guessed that the African Magician had got the Magic Lamp and used it to carry away his Palace and all in it, he did not know how he could possibly regain it. Indeed his mind became numb, all hope left him, and after three frantic days he decided that death was the only way out of his troubles. So he went out of the city to where the river plunged over the rocks down into a deep chasm and decided to fling himself into it.

First of all, however, he knelt down and clasped his hands in prayer to Allah the All-Merciful.

As he did so he rubbed the ring which the African Magician had given him long ago, and which he had completely forgotten.

At once the Jinnee of the Ring who had saved him from the underground hall, appeared before him and said:

'What are thy commands? I am ready to obey thee as thy slave, as the slave of the man who has the Magic Ring on his finger – both I and the other Slaves of the Ring!'

'Noble Jinnee, save my life a second time!' cried Aladdin. 'Bring back my Palace and with it my wife the Princess Badroulboudour!'

'What you ask is beyond my power,' answered the Jinnee. 'I am only the Slave of the Ring, and the Slaves of the Lamp are mightier than I.'

'If that is so,' said Aladdin, 'I command you simply to transport me to the spot where my Palace is, wherever in the world it may be, and set me down under the window of the Princess Badroulboudour.'

As soon as he had spoken the Jinnee took him up and carried

him in a moment to the furthest confines of Africa, and set him down below a window of his own Palace.

Very soon the Princess discovered who was there, and eagerly let him in by the secret door in the wall below her rooms.

As soon as they had greeted one another, Aladdin asked what had become of the Magic Lamp, and the Princess fell on her knees before him weeping, and sobbed:

'My Prince, the blame is mine. This wicked Magician came to the Palace offering new lamps in exchange for old ones, and I gave him the Magic Lamp not knowing its power, but thinking it was only a worthless old lamp which you chanced to have left on the shelf in your room.'

'Mine is the fault,' answered Aladdin. 'I should either have told you the virtues of the Lamp, or else I should have locked it away in a safe place where none but I could find it. But tell me now of this evil Magician and what harm he has done to you since he obtained the Magic Lamp.'

'None yet, save to carry me and the Palace here into the utmost confines of Africa,' answered the Princess. 'But you have arrived only just in time. Each day he visits me and begs me to become his wife willingly – and I always refuse. To-morrow he comes to ask me for the last time – and if I refuse he will make me his by force.'

'Then do not refuse,' said Aladdin, thinking swiftly. 'Answer him with soft words: say that as you know you will never see me again, you are ready to become his wife. But when he comes to drink the Bridal Cup with you, make sure that you drop into it the powder that I shall give you – and make doubly sure that you only pretend to drink from it before you hand it to him.'

When day dawned Aladdin hid himself in his own room – where he rubbed the Magic Ring and obtained from the Jinnee of the Ring what he needed.

Meanwhile the African Magician had come to visit the Princess, and was overjoyed at her change of heart. He had no suspicion of any ill, for he had quite forgotten about the Magic Ring, and was certain that Aladdin had no means of following him.

'I go to make ready for our wedding!' he cried triumphantly. 'Tonight we shall be wed, and tomorrow, with the aid of this Magic Lamp which I carry in my robe I will make us Emperor and Empress of the whole world!'

When he returned as the sun was setting, he was clad from head to foot in cloth of gold embroidered with jewels. At his command slaves set out a great banquet on golden dishes, with wines in jewelled flasks, and then left him alone with the Princess.

'And now!' he cried, 'let us drink from the Bridal Cup and seal our union for ever!'

The Princess took the Cup in one hand, raising her veil a little way with the other, and made pretence to drink. Then she flung back her veil altogether as she handed the Cup to the Magician and leant towards him, her beautiful eyes full of passion.

With a cry of triumph the Magician took the Bridal Cup and drained it at a draught. He looked into her eyes – and all the false passion had turned to hatred and loathing. Then he knew how he had been tricked, and as Aladdin stepped from behind the curtain where he had been hidden, the poison did its work, and with a terrible cry the African Magician fell back dead.

Swiftly Aladdin snatched the Magic Lamp from the body of his enemy and exclaimed: 'Leave me a moment, my Princess, and return when I call!'

As soon as she had gone he rubbed the Magic Lamp and the Jinnee appeared bowing and said:

'What are thy commands? I am ready to obey thee as thy

slave, and the slave of any that holds the Lamp in his hands –
I and the other Slaves of the Lamp!'

'Noble Jinnee,' cried Aladdin, 'I command you and your
fellow Slaves of the Lamp to take up this Palace with everything living and dead that is within it, and transport it back
instantly to the exact spot in China whence it was brought.'

The Jinnee bowed and vanished. And a moment later he
and the other Jinn of the Lamp had carried the Palace back to
the Sultan's park so smoothly that no one in it felt more than
two tiny jars as it was taken up and set down.

Next morning the Sultan looked sadly out of his window –
and cried aloud in sudden delight. Not many minutes later he
and the Grand Vizier and several of his court were on their
way to Aladdin's Palace. And soon he was embracing his
daughter the Princess Badroulboudour and looking with
horror upon the dead body of the African Magician – which
he at once commanded should be taken and thrown on the
nearest dunghill for the vultures and jackals to devour.

And after this Aladdin and his wife lived safely and happily
in their Palace, and in time succeeded the Sultan and reigned
gloriously for very many years.

Merlin, the Wizard of Britain

IN the days when the Roman Empire was falling and the legions were withdrawn from Britain, there was a King called Vortigern who tried to protect his kingdom from the Saxon invaders by inviting other Saxons to settle in Britain and keep the invaders out.

This worked very well for some years; but at length the two Saxon leaders, Hengist and Horsa, made war on Vortigern and conquered much of his land for themselves. Vortigern tried to make a treaty with Hengist, but the best and bravest of the Britons were murdered unarmed at a peace conference on Salisbury Plain, and the Saxons went on with their conquests.

The people of Britain murmured against Vortigern, and secretly invited the rightful king, Aurelius Ambrosius, who was in exile, to return and free them, and bring with him his brother Uther Pendragon. Vortigern discovered or suspected something of this and decided to build himself a castle in the mountains of Wales so strong that in it he could never be taken.

But when a spot was chosen on the hill of Dinas Emrys, and the builders began to lay the foundation stones, it was found that there was something strange and uncanny about the place. For whatever stones were laid down in the daytime were swallowed up by the ground during the hours of darkness so that next day there was not a trace of them to be found. And yet the flat stretch of ground near the hill-top seemed to be as firm and unstirred as before they began their labours.

When he heard this, Vortigern sent for his magicians, and they came to Dinas Emrys and began to practise their arts of divination. Very soon they discovered something far different from what they expected to find; it was revealed to them that a child who was no man's son would be able to tell how the castle could be built – but that he would also cause their deaths.

So, after consulting together, they went to the King and said:

'The castle of Dinas Emrys, the strong castle that you desire to build, can only be built if the mortar between the stones is mixed with the blood of a child who is no man's son. Our advice is that you send messengers throughout the kingdom until they find such a child, slay him, and bring his blood to you in a sealed jar.'

This seemed good to Vortigern, and the messengers were sent out. Before long they came to a town which was later known as Caermerlin and overheard some children quarrelling. And one boy shouted at another:

'How dare you argue with me! I am a prince, and both my father and mother were princes. But as for you – why, everyone knows that you are no man's son!'

When the messengers heard this, they immediately seized the boy and asked him who he was, and why his companion had jeered at him for being 'no man's son'.

'My name is Merlin,' answered the boy, 'and I know that you have come from King Vortigern to kill me because of a false prophecy. His magicians have cheated him – and wish my death, because I alone know why the stones of Dinas Emrys sink into the ground each night, and my knowledge will bring them to their death if the King finds my words to be true and theirs false. Now my advice to you is that you take me living to Vortigern – or else you yourselves may not return living to tell him how I escaped from you.'

Amazed by the boy Merlin's knowledge, the messengers agreed to take him with them still living, if he would save them from Vortigern's anger.

'Tell him all you have seen and heard – and will see and hear on the way,' answered Merlin, 'and he will not blame but rather reward you for bringing me to him living.'

So they set out for Dinas Emrys, and in the first village through which they passed they saw a man come out of a shop carrying a piece of leather and saying: 'With this I shall be able to mend my shoes, and then I'll be able to walk in them for many years to come.'

When Merlin heard this, he laughed, and when the messengers asked him why, he replied:

'Because that man will die today – before he even reaches his house.'

Curious to see if the young magician could indeed see into the future, two of the messengers followed the man. And sure enough, half-way up the hill to his home he suddenly clapped his hand to his side and sank down dead through heart-failure.

After several other such demonstrations as this, the messengers had no doubt at all that the boy Merlin could indeed see into the future better than any magician in Vortigern's court.

When they reached Dinas Emrys, and the messengers had told Vortigern of all Merlin's prophecies which had been shown to be true, the King said:

'But what is the meaning of my magician's vision – and your companion's jibe – that you are "no man's son"?'

'That is true,' answered Merlin. 'My father was an incubus – an evil spirit which visited my mother as she slept. Do not be afraid: I am no devil, but a mortal man – the greatest of the Magicians of the Isle of Britain. Nor will I risk my salvation more than any sinful man born of woman, provided I use my magic arts only for good and not for evil – that the magic I practise be White Magic and not Black Magic . . . Now, as to what stirs the ground each night: if your magicians cannot tell you what is below this stretch of ground, it seems to me that they are of little account – and if they affirm that only my blood can cement the building, then it seems that they lie.'

Vortigern questioned his magicians sharply as to what was beneath the ground, but they could not answer.

Then said Merlin: 'Beneath the ground is a pool of water which causes the foundations to sink. Dig and see.' When Vortigern's labourers had dug down they indeed uncovered a pool of dark water. And Merlin said: 'Can your magicians tell what lies below the pool and causes the water to shake and sink the foundations?' When they could not answer this either, Merlin said: 'Command that the pool be drained and below it you will find two stone chests in which sleep two dragons. Every night these dragons awake, break out of the chests, and fight. Their battle stirs the waters of the pool and causes the foundations of the castle to sink.'

When the pool was drained all was revealed just as Merlin had said – and the magicians were immediately executed by order of King Vortigern as liars and cheats.

After this the castle could be built safely, and Vortigern asked Merlin to prophesy his future.

'If you can escape the fires lit by Aurelius Ambrosius and Uther Pendragon, the sons of Constantine who was the rightful king whom you caused to be murdered, you will live out your life,' answered Merlin. 'But you cannot do so. They land tomorrow at Totnes and soon Aurelius shall reign, until poison ends his life; and after him the Pendragon. He shall be the father of Arthur, the greatest king that Britain shall ever have.'

Hearing this, Vortigern imprisoned Merlin in the new castle of Dinas Emrys and marched to meet the two sons of Constantine who landed next day with an army of ten thousand men at Totnes. But the Britons were tired of Vortigern and his policies, and blamed him for the death of all their lords and princes whom Hengist had murdered on Salisbury Plain. So they deserted to Aurelius Ambrosius, the rightful King. Vortigern fled with a few followers to a strong tower on the borders of Wales not far from Gloucester, but Ambrosius besieged it and, being unable to break in, bunt it to the ground and Vortigern with it.

The first act of the new King was to attack the Saxons, and a great battle was fought in which Hengist was taken and slain.

It took several years, however, to restore Britain to peace and security. When at length the land seemed safe from unexpected rebellions and further Saxon invasions (though the Saxons still held part of the north and east of the country), Aurelius Ambrosius decided to build a great monument to the British lords and princes who had been murdered by Hengist on Salisbury Plain.

While he was discussing plans with his architects, none of whom seemed able to produce any worthy scheme, Tremounus the Bishop of Caerleon came to him and said:

'If anyone living can devise a fitting monument, that man is Merlin who prophesied Vortigern's death and your victory. Vortigern imprisoned him in Dinas Emrys, and there he dwells to this day, and has made the castle his own.'

King Ambrosius sent at once for Merlin. But when he and his lords saw how young a man claimed to be the great Magician, they expressed some doubt in his powers. To test him one young lord asked Merlin how he would meet his death.

'You will break your neck falling from your horse,' answered Merlin shortly, 'and your death will come upon you on the third day from now.'

Rather alarmed, but still doubting, the young lord disguised himself carefully and came next day to ask Merlin the same question.

'You will be strangled,' answered Merlin, 'and your death will come upon you on the second day from now.'

Certain that he had tricked the Magician, the young lord appeared blithely before him the next day, heavily disguised as an old man, and asked the same question.

'You will be drowned tomorrow,' answered Merlin shortly, and turned away as if in disgust.

Then the young lord tore off his disguise, and he and the others mocked Merlin as a cheat, who had betrayed his false pretences to magic by not knowing that it was the same man who had asked the question each time, and giving three different answers – two at least of which must be untrue.

'What I have said, I have said, and what I have said is true,' was all that Merlin would answer. Next day the young lord rode out hunting with the King and all the rest of the Court. Suddenly as he galloped along a narrow path high over a sheer cliff above a raging river his horse took fright, reared, swerved, lost its footing and fell with its rider into the stream. As they went over the edge, the young man tried to spring clear; but the reins caught round his neck and hanged him a moment before horse and man struck a deep pool in the river where they sank at once and were drowned.

After this, and a few other examples of his power, no one doubted that Merlin was as great a Magician as Bishop Tremounus had said.

Accordingly King Ambrosius asked him about the monument to the murdered princes, and Merlin answered:

'In Ireland, on the mountain of Killaraus stands a great and mystical monument: some call it the Etins' Circle and others the Giants' Dance. It is made of stone and there is no other such building anywhere in the world. It is made of huge stones of great virtue – for they have the virtue of healing the sick. The stones as I say are of enormous size: there is no man living who can move them, however strong he be.'

'Merlin,' answered the King, 'you speak strangely. You say

there is no man born who can move these stones, and yet you bid me bring them from Ireland.'

'Magic art is more powerful than the mere strength of men,' said Merlin, 'and I will help you to bring the Giants' Dance to Salisbury Plain. Send now an army to Ireland, with your brother Uther Pendragon in command of it – and soon you will have a worthy monument to your friends, and one beneath whose shadow you yourself may lie when your time comes.'

So Uther Pendragon set out for Ireland with an army; defeated King Gillomanius who tried to prevent him from his attempt, and came to the hill of Killaraus on which stood a circle of gigantic stones standing upright and supporting a ring of stones laid and fitted above them.

'There is the Giants' Dance, the ring of stones which the Giants brought from Africa in ancient days,' said Merlin. 'Try now whether you and all your men can move them.'

Then all Uther's men advanced and set to work, labouring with all their might. But they could not stir a single one of the stones.

So Merlin came forward once more and cried:

'Uther Pendragon, draw back, you and all your men, and stand ready. Watch, but do not stir until I bid you each to take hold of a stone.'

Uther and his men drew back, and Merlin went from stone to stone of the great circle, touching each one in turn and chanting an incantation. At length he had charmed each stone in the circle, and drew back, crying:

'Come quickly now, Uther, with all your men, and take up these stones. Leave not one behind, for now they will seem to you as light as feather balls. And now, with due care, you may carry them every one to your ships and sail away to Britain.'

The men advanced once more. And now, under Merlin's charm, they found each stone so light that four men could carry them easily down the mountain and across the plain to their ships.

And the stones remained mere featherweights while they brought them to Britain, to the plain near Amesbury where Hengist's men had stabbed the bravest of the Britons with their long knives. Here they set them up, under Merlin's guidance, just as they had been when the Giants first built their Dance in Ireland.

Then Merlin cried aloud a Word of Power, and the full weight returned to the stones so that they settled in the earth and were embedded so firmly that they remain to this day almost as Merlin left them. But, by his command, the name of the great Circle was changed from the Giant's Dance to Stonehenge.

And Stonehenge soon became the tomb of Aurelius Ambrosius, as Merlin had foreseen. For Pascent, a son of Vortigern, escaped to Germany and brought over a fresh army of Saxons. King Ambrosius was able to defeat these, but one of them came disguised to his court and poisoned him.

After Aurelius Ambrosius was laid to rest in Stonehenge, his brother Uther Pendragon came to the throne. He was able to keep the Saxons at bay, and to overcome and kill Octa, the son of Hengist.

But peace did not come to poor, war-torn Britain, even when the Saxons were defeated, or held at bay. Gorlois, Duke of Cornwall, had a beautiful wife called Ygerne. When he brought her to Caerleon at the time when all the Dukes of Britain came to do homage to Uther Pendragon, the King looked upon her beauty and fell madly in love with her.

He tried to tempt her to desert her husband for him, but Ygerne repulsed him with scorn, and told Duke Gorlois all that had passed between them. In fury, Gorlois left the Court, taking his wife with him, and paid no attention to his liege lord the King's commands for him to return to Caerleon.

Thereupon Uther Pendragon raised an army and marched into Cornwall, swearing to slay his rebellious subject and scatter his forces. But Gorlois did not risk a pitched battle: instead, he left Ygerne safely guarded in his strongest castle of Tintagel on a great rock sticking out into the sea, and fortified himself in his scarcely less impregnable castle of Dimilioc.

Uther laid siege to this castle. But after a while he realized that he had little chance of taking either it or Tintagel without many months of siege. He could not rest on account of his love for Ygerne, and at last he told his passion to his friend the Welsh prince Elphin, who at once advised him to seek Merlin's help and advice.

Merlin, who was one of the few Magicians who could see into the future and help to mould events yet to be, saw the great good that would come to Britain from Uther's sinful passion for Ygerne, and said to the King:

'I will help you to achieve that which you desire if you will promise to grant me whatever I may ask, so be that you can grant it with honour.'

Uther agreed to this, binding himself with the most solemn oaths, and Merlin then brewed a magic potion which he gave Uther to drink, and to Elphin, and drinking also of it himself. And at once their forms and likenesses were changed so that Uther seemed to be turned into Gorlois his very self, and Merlin and Elphin into his two most trusted Knights.

'In this likeness,' said Merlin, 'we may enter Tintagel as the Duke and his friends, with a feigned tale, and none will know the difference – no, not even Ygerne when you, my lord King, clasp her in your arms – as it is said that Paris the Trojan clasped fair Helen when he came to her in the likeness of her husband Menelaus and led her away to Troy. But one thing you must remember: it is necessary that we be out of the Castle of Tintagel before the sun rises tomorrow.'

So the three of them went boldly up to Tintagel; and the guards let them in without question, thinking that the Duke had stolen away from Dimilioc to see his wife. Nor did Ygerne have any doubt that it was Gorlois her husband who came to visit her that night, and slipped away so silently before daylight came.

As Uther and his two companions, still wearing the magical likeness of Gorlois and his friends, came to the gate of Tintagel, the Knight in command of the guard looked at him with surprise and exclaimed:

'My lord Duke, this is indeed marvellous. Not an hour ago news came that you had been slain last night, making a surprise foray from Castle Dimilioc into King Uther's camp!'

'You see that the news was false,' said the false Duke Gorlois. 'I did indeed leave Dimilioc – but only to come here to Tintagel to visit my lady, Ygerne.'

Nevertheless Uther found that the news was true when he reached his own camp. But by that time the sun had risen, and he and Merlin and Elphin had returned to their own shapes.

With the death of Gorlois the war came to an end, and as a pledge of peace and forgiveness Uther made haste to marry Ygerne. But when their first child was about to be born Merlin came to Uther and said:

'Fulfil now your promise. I ask that when your son is born you give him to me to carry away and bring up in secret. For troubles loom over this land, and only if I protect him can this child survive to grow up and become the greatest and most famous King this land shall ever know – whose name shall be Arthur.'

All came about as Merlin foretold. When the child was born Merlin carried him out of dark Tintagel at dead of night and hid him away until he was grown into a handsome young man.

When this time came Uther had been poisoned by the Saxons who were again overrunning the land, and the Britons could do nothing against them since they kept quarrelling among themselves as to who should be their King.

But as soon as the time was ripe Merlin advised the Archbishop to call together all the would-be rulers of the land, with their barons and their knights, to a great service in London on Christmas Day. And when the service was ended they came out of the abbey church of Westminster to find in the Churchyard a sword sticking point downwards in a great block of stone. And set in the stone were letters of gold which read: 'Whoso pulleth out this sword from this stone is the true-born King of all Britain.'

All tried in vain to pull out the sword, but only a young man called Arthur, who was squire to a Knight called Sir Ector, could do so. And at length Merlin proved to them that this Arthur was the only son of King Uther Pendragon and of Ygerne – told of how his life began strangely in dark Tintagel by the Cornish sea, and of how he had cared for the child and set him to grow up in the household of Sir Ector.

So Arthur became King. And by his own valour and with Merlin's help he defeated the Saxons in twelve pitched battles, and the last – that of Mons Badonicus – brought peace to Britain for all the rest of his long and prosperous reign. And that peace was only broken when the traitor Mordred fought against him and brought about his end with his own death on the tragic field of Camlann.

But Merlin did not live to see this day, for before it dawned he fell victim to an enchantment stronger than any among his own magic lore – the enchantment of love.

After King Arthur had been reigning for many years and Merlin was growing old, there came to the court at Camelot a beautiful damsel called Niviene, whom some named Nimue or Vivian.

At once Merlin's wisdom forsook him, and he fell madly in love with Niviene. But she scorned him and in time grew to hate him. For he would follow her about everywhere, and she could not escape from him.

To begin with this did not displease her overmuch, for she persuaded Merlin to teach her some of his magic though she never learnt to foretell the future as he could.

One day he told her of the story of the Lake of Diane which lay in the mysterious Forest of En-Val, and how Diane had fled from Faunus, and been overtaken there, but cheated him into entering a tomb under the ground and then filled it with molten lead and so burying him yet alive.

'But this cruelty did her little good,' concluded Merlin, 'for Felix, the friend of Faunus, found out what Diane had done, and smote off her head with a single blow of his sword. However, the tomb of Faunus may still be seen, and any who sleeps upon it sees strange visions of an enchanted palace haunted by the spirits of Faunus and Diane.'

'I would like to visit this place,' said Niviene.

'Do not ask me to lead you there,' begged Merlin, 'for I know that my end will come upon me in the Forest of En-Val, and I too shall pass living into my tomb. But who shall place me there, or how it shall come to pass, I cannot see. For only by Black Magic could I learn how to change my own fate – and Black Magic have I never used, nor will I even to save my life. For though I might keep my life in my body for many hundreds of years by Black Magic, yet if I did so, in the end I would lose both body and soul to the Powers of Darkness.'

Nevertheless Niviene begged Merlin to take her to the Forest of En-Val, promising that she would be his love if he built her a palace there and performed other enchantments that she would ask of him. And Merlin was so besotted in his love that he could not resist her, and together they set out.

Many adventures befell them on the way, but at length they

came to the Forest of En-Val. It was set about with steep hills, and they came to it through a narrow valley at the end of which, where the Forest began, they saw chairs of ebony and gold set on either side of the way, and protected from the rain with an arch of ivory. In the chairs sat two men holding harps in their hands.

'Stay!' exclaimed Merlin when he saw them. 'Yonder sit the Enchanters of En-Val. Any who hears the music of their harps falls to the ground as if overcome with sleep. And very soon that sleep passes into death, if the enchantment be not broken. But I am here to protect you, and will try my powers on these evil men. Remain here until they fall – or until I perish in the attempt.'

So saying he stuffed his ears with lumps of beeswax and advanced boldly towards the enchanters.

As Merlin approached them, the two enchanters raised their harps and began to pluck at the strings. As the unearthly music floated up the valley, Niviene and her attendants slipped from their horses and sank to the ground in a deep sleep.

But Merlin walked steadily forward, and cried: 'For the deaths you have caused to so many, and for the pain and fear you are even now causing to my fair sweet love and her attendants, I bring you a terrible punishment!'

So saying he raised his arms and spoke a great, resounding charm. At it the thunder pealed in the clear sky – and the two enchanters sank back into their chairs, the harps falling from their hands and slipping to the ground. Merlin spoke again, and it seemed that all power to move went from the two enchanters, and they lolled back in their chairs as if they had been babies.

Then Merlin turned swiftly to Niviene and raised her to her feet – and she cried aloud suddenly and clung to Merlin for the first time in her life.

'Oh, I have been on the edge of death!' she cried. 'I felt its very pains – pains as if the ministers of Hell were tearing my flesh!'

'All will be well now,' answered Merlin. And when the attendants had recovered too he bade them dig two deep holes and set in them the chairs with the enchanters in them. Then he filled the holes with a flame of fire, and caused them to be covered over with earth.

'So shall they remain until the day when King Arthur lands in Avalon!' he said solemnly. 'Not a hair of their heads shall be destroyed by the fire until that day: but when that day dawns the fire will consume them, their chairs and their magic harps to ashes. Let this be a proof that I was the greatest Wizard of Britain! For now my end draws near.'

After this they went on into the Forest of En-Val and came at last to the Tomb of Faunus – a great slab of stone that twenty men could scarcely lift, set upon other stones that raised it a little from the ground.

Merlin spoke a spell, and the stone rose slowly. Beneath it a stairway led steeply down into the rock. Lighting a lamp, Merlin took Niviene by the hand and led her down into a mysterious chamber in the heart of the rock. On a stone table in the middle of this cave lay a body covered with a cloak.

'There lies Faunus,' said Merlin. 'But when I draw the cloak away he will turn into dust.'

This befell as he said, and soon the dust that had been Faunus floated away as Merlin shook the cloak.

'And what of the beautiful palace where Faunus and Diane still dwell as spirits?' asked Niviene.

'To enter it we must sleep here upon the table of stone,' answered Merlin. 'For only two lovers may enter that palace in the spirit.'

Now Niviene saw a way to be rid of Merlin for ever. So she pretended that at last his love had conquered her, and she had fallen in love with him.

And she spoke such sweet words, mingled with charms that she had learnt from Merlin, that very soon the old magician fell into a deep sleep there upon the stone table.

Then Niviene tiptoed out of the vault and up the narrow steps, out into the Forest of En-Val. When she was outside, she turned and spoke the spell which Merlin had used to raise the stone – and the stone sank back slowly until it covered the entrance to the tomb of Faunus – which had now become the tomb of Merlin – as if it had never been raised.

And there Merlin the Wizard of Britain sleeps until such time as a greater magic raises him once more to aid Britain in its hour of greatest need.

Bradamante and the Wizard

In the days when Charlemagne was Emperor of France there lived a beautiful maiden called Bradamante, who was sister to one of the great Paladins, Rinaldo. She was brought up as befitted the daughter of a great Lord of Christendom, but from her earliest youth her chief joy was in feats of arms, and her greatest delight to mount the most fiery horses in her father's stable.

She grew up very tall and strong, as well as fair to see, and it soon became her custom to put on man's armour and take part in jousts and tournaments – in which she usually carried off the prize, against all comers.

Naturally so beautiful and unusual a maiden had no lack of wooers, but Bradamante listened to none save the noble knight Roger, who had quitted the Moorish service to fight for Charlemagne in the cause of Christendom. But she kept silence as to her love and was content to wait until such time as Roger should think fit to claim her as his bride.

Suddenly the tidings came to her that Roger had vanished from among men, no one knew whither. As was her wont, Bradamante heard and said nothing. But next day she sharpened her sword, buckled on her armour, and set off to see if perchance some ill had befallen him.

After many adventures she found a young knight seated on a hillside with his head in his hands and weeping bitterly. She stopped to comfort him and see if she could help him in his sorrow, and he said:

'I have lost my beloved. As we rode together on our way to the court of Charlemagne, there came an evil Wizard in black armour, riding upon a dragon, who snatched her away from me and carried her to his castle.'

'Have you not tried to rescue her from this Wizard?' asked Bradamante.

'I tried but lately to enter the castle,' said the knight, 'and I had the help of two noble warriors called Gradasso, king of Sericane, and that valiant Paladin the young knight Roger, who had also come to fight the Wizard. When they heard how my beloved lady had been carried off by him, their eagerness redoubled, and they vied with one another as to who should strike the first blow to set her free. When we came to the Wizard's castle it was Gradasso who first seized the horn which hangs beside his gate and blew a blast that rang through the castle.

'A moment later the winged dragon on which the Wizard rode shot up into the sky above the castle walls, and on its back the Wizard in his black armour with a great round shield upon his arm covered with a silken cloth. Down he swooped and struck with his spear now at Gradasso, now at brave Roger; but they struck back, though most of their blows fell harmlessly upon the dragon's scales, while every thrust of the Wizard's spear wounded either one or the other. Yet neither brave knight would retreat an inch; and at last the Wizard drew the silken cover from his shield: the whole blazing sun seemed to be reflected in it, blazing, dazzling and terrible. It seared me to the very brain, and I fell to the ground and remembered no more until I awoke to find myself alone here upon the mountainside – though how I came to be so far from the Wizard's castle I cannot tell.'

'And Roger?' asked Bradamante anxiously.

'Roger and Gradasso have doubtless been carried off by the Wizard to the dark prison cells beneath his castle,' answered the knight, 'the cells in which my beloved lady lies prisoner also. And alas, I can do nothing, alone and wounded as I am, to save them.'

Now it chanced that this knight was none other than Pinabello, the false son of a false race, whose one wish in life was to destroy as many of the knights of Charlemagne as he could. Bradamante had no idea of this, and readily consented when Pinabello offered to lead her to the castle of the Wizard.

'If you desire to visit that terrible place,' he said, 'I will show you the way. But remember that I have warned you of its dangers. Even if you manage to climb those walls of steel you will find yourself the Wizard's prisoner like the rest.'

'I care nothing for the risk,' said Bradamante. 'Lead on. It cannot be that God will suffer the powers of evil to triumph over our holy cause: however hopeless our case may seem, still I believe that Roger and Gradasso will yet be freed from the Wizard's power.'

These words only made Pinabello the more determined to bring about Bradamante's death as soon as possible. So he set off with her through the forest, and before long he had decided on his plan of action.

Turning aside from the main path he led her deep into the darkest parts of the forest where it was broken by huge rocks and chasms near the base of the mountains. Presently Pinabello stopped by the side of a dark gulch overhung with trees and brambles.

'This is the place I was seeking,' he said. 'At the bottom of this cleft in the rocks is a passage which is said to lead up through the cliffs and into the Wizard's castle. It is just too deep for one person to drop into. But if we cut a long branch from one of those oak trees, I can hold one end and lower you until you reach the floor of the cavern beneath out of which the passage leads.'

Suspecting nothing, Bradamante agreed to this. Very soon the branch was cut and Pinabello was holding on to the top of it while she clambered carefully down.

But as soon as she was near to the bottom of the branch Pinabello shouted gleefully:

'I hope you can jump! It's a long way to the bottom!' and let go of his end of the branch, giving it a good push at the same time so as to send it well out from the side of the gulch.

It was a long fall, and Bradamante would surely have been killed when she struck the floor of the cavern. But by a lucky chance the branch turned over as she fell so that it struck the bottom first, and though it smashed to pieces, she came down through its twigs and smaller branches which broke her fall.

Nevertheless she lay for some time stunned. And when she recovered it took her a little while to recover from the shock; and although no bones were broken, she was badly bruised and shaken.

At last she was able to set out down the cave, hoping to find some way out, though she was sure that the wicked Pinabello

had deceived her and that there was no passage leading into the Wizard's castle.

In this she was right. But she was more fortunate than she dreamed – and Pinabello could not have chosen a worse place for his wicked attempt to murder her. For presently she saw a light at the end of the chasm, and came to a kind of chapel where dwelt none other than the good enchantress Melissa who welcomed her kindly.

When Melissa had attended to Bradamante's many scratches and bruises, and given her food and wine, she asked how she chanced to be wandering alone and wounded in the dark and secret chasm.

So Bradamante told her all the story, and when she had finished, Melissa said:

'You are lucky to have escaped so easily from that dastardly craven Pinabello, and to have been helped by him to achieve the very thing he wanted least: to have found me and gained my aid. But as for the Wizard, no man, however brave, can withstand him, with his magic mirror and the dragon who is his flying steed. If you would reach Roger, you must get possession of the Ring which was stolen from Angelica, the beautiful witch of the East who came to France to ensnare the brave Orlando and save the Paynim hosts from defeat. Whosoever holds this ring in his mouth becomes invisible; and whoso wears it upon his finger is safe from any magic charm or spell. Agramante the African king stole it from Angelica, and he gave it to Brunello the dwarf, who has it still. He rides only a few miles from here, and you must get it from him by stealth.'

'How fortunate I am that Brunello is so near at hand,' said Bradamante. 'But tell me how I shall know him when we meet.'

'He is of low stature,' answered Melissa, 'and covered with black hair; his nose lies flat upon his face, and his skin is

yellow, as the skin is of those who come from the far lands beyond Scythia. You must engage him in talk about magic and enchantment, and lead him on to offering himself as a guide to the Wizard's castle. But if he shows any signs of putting the Magic Ring into his mouth, strike him dead immediately, and take it from him. And above all do not let him know who you are or why you want to visit the Wizard's castle.'

Next morning Melissa supplied Bradamante with a horse and brought her out on to the open plain near a village not far from the mountains among which the Wizard had his Castle.

Following Melissa's advice, Bradamante stabled her horse at the inn and entered the parlour, where she found Brunello drinking among several boon companions.

One glance showed Bradamante that she had already met Brunello in the lists at several tournaments in the castles of France – and one glance told Brunello the same story: but each pretended never to have seen the other before.

So they fell into talk about castles, and the knights who lay imprisoned therein. And naturally the subject of the Wizard's castle and the captives in his dungeons soon cropped up, Bradamante feigning to know little about the matter and to be hearing of it for the first time, and Brunello feigning a belief in her ignorance.

'Many an adventure as perilous have I dared,' said Bradamante at length, 'and never yet have I failed to trample my foe under my feet. So if our worthy host will give me a guide, I myself will challenge the Wizard to deadly combat and see whether I can rescue those noble knights whom you say are his prisoners.'

Brunello declared that he would suffer no man else to be her guide, but would himself lead Bradamante to the Wizard's castle. So they rode out together until they came up the mountain to the very foot of the castle.

'Look at those walls of steel that crown the precipice,' began Brunello turning his back on Bradamante for the first time. Before he could say more, or turn back to her, a strong girdle was passed round his arms and they were fastened tightly to his sides: and in spite of his cries and struggles Bradamante drew the Ring off his finger and placed it on her own, though kill him she would not.

Then she raised the horn which hung from a cord by the castle gates, and blowing a long, loud blast, waited calmly for the Wizard to answer.

Soon he appeared on his flying steed, bearing on his left arm the silken-covered magic shield, while he uttered spells and incantations that had laid low many a knight and lady. But, with the Magic Ring on her finger, Bradamante was able to listen calmly to them all, and was no whit the worse even for the blackest of them.

Furious at his defeat, the Wizard snatched the silken cover from his shield and flashed it towards Bradamante. Knowing full well what was wont to follow, Bradamante sank to the ground and lay there as if a victim to the enchantment. At this the Wizard covered his shield once more and guided his steed swiftly to where the maiden lay. Then, unclasping a chain from his waist he bent down to fasten it about her.

As he did so Bradamante suddenly held the Magic Ring in front of his eyes, and the Wizard staggered back and stood before her, a helpless old man with white hair and a face wrinkled with age and sorrow. In vain he tried to excuse himself, saying that he had protected Roger many years ago and now only held him captive so as to keep him from roaming into further dangers.

'I built this castle and filled it full with all manner of good things only for him,' he ended. 'And all the knights and ladies whom I have taken prisoner I have kept only to be companions for him in his captivity.'

But Bradamante would not listen. Taking up the Magic Shield and slipping it on to her arm, she bade the Wizard lead the way into the castle.

When they reached the top of the long flight of steps Bradamante pointed to a stone in the floor graven with many strange and magical signs: 'Raise that!' she said.

Then, because there was no escape from the powers of the Ring and the Shield, the Wizard raised the stone, revealing a deep vault in the centre of which, immediately below the hole through which they were looking, stood a great earthenware pot in which burnt a magic flame.

Bradamante stretched out the hand with the Ring on it suddenly and with a cry the Wizard let fall the stone so that it fell through the hole and right on to the flame beneath.

There was a sound of thunder, and a rumbling crash as if all the rocks on earth were falling together. Then came a blinding flash; and when Bradamante could see again the Wizard and his castle had vanished for ever, and in their place on the pleasant, grassy hillside, stood a troop of knights and ladies who had been his prisoners.

At their head was Roger, whole and unhurt – and for a little while Bradamante saw and heard none but he.

The Franklin's Tale

Retold from *Chaucer*

ELEANOR FARJEON

THERE was once a knight who lived and loved in Armorica, which we call Britain. He loved a lady, and performed many a labour before he won her. She was the fairest under the sun, and came of a noble family, so that he lacked the courage to tell her how he loved her. But her eye had fallen upon him, and she had determined secretly to take him for her lord and master – or such mastery as men may have over their wives! And when he knew her mind, he swore by his knighthood never to master her against her will, or to be jealous of her, but to obey her in all things like a lover. And she thanked him, saying, 'Sir, since in your goodness you grant me so much, I will be your own true humble wife till my heart stops beating.' And so they were at perfect ease together. For sirs, let me tell you this: love between friends will not be constrained by force, when force comes in, love takes to his wings. For love is a spirit, and must be free; and women, as well as men, desire their liberty. And so, her servant in love and her lord in marriage, the knight took his wife home to his own country, not far from Penmark; where, for a year or so, they lived in bliss.

Then, so the story goes, this knight, who was called Arviragus, was set on going to England for a year or two, to seek honour by deeds of arms. When he had departed, Dorigen his wife, who loved him as her heart's life, spent the time in weeping and sighing; she longed for him so much that the world was nothing to her. Her friends tried to comfort her, and begged her to give over her sorrow; and when in time letters came from Arviragus, telling of his welfare, her grief lessened a little, and she consented once more to leave her room, and go roaming in their company.

Her castle stood close to the sea, and now she often walked on the cliff with her friends, watching the ships and barges sailing the ocean; and Dorigen would say to herself, 'Is there no ship among all I see that will bring me home my lord?'

At other times she would sit gazing down upon the grim black rocks, and her heart would quake for fear, and she would say, 'Almighty God, why, among all thy works, didst thou create the rocks? The dreadful rocks have slain a hundred thousand bodies of mankind! For my dear husband's sake, I would all rocks were sunk as deep as Hell. These rocks destroy my heart with fear.' And then she would weep bitterly.

Her friends, finding the sea saddened her, devised sports for her elsewhere, by springs and rivers, and other delightful spots; where they danced, and played at chess and back-gammon. One morning early they went forth to spend the whole day in a garden, where food had been provided; the month of May had painted with soft showers the flowers and leaves, and man's craft had so laid out the garden that it was a paradise of scents and colours. After their dinner, they began to dance and sing in the pleasaunce; but Dorigen went apart and sang of her sorrow that her husband was absent.

Among the dancers was a young Squire, as fresh and gay as the month of May itself. He sang and danced better than any man since the beginning of the world; he was indeed in all things one of the best endowed men alive, young, strong, and virtuous, and well-beloved. And all unknown to Dorigen, this Squire, who was called Aurelius, had loved her for two years above all women; but he had never dared to tell her so. Only he composed many songs and roundelays of how he languished for her love, as Echo did for Narcissus, which he would sing in her hearing; and in the dance he would look pleadingly at her, as one who asks for a favour, yet she never guessed his meaning.

But on this day it happened that they talked together, for she had long known and liked him as her neighbour; and when Aurelius saw his chance, he spoke to his purpose.

'Madam, if it had been pleasing to you, I would that the day your Arviragus went to sea I had gone too, and never returned again. For I know well that my love for you is vain, and my only reward will be a broken heart. Madam, take pity on my pain, for you can slay me or spare me as with a sword. Would I could die here at your feet! I can say no more, but if you do not have mercy on me, sweet, I shall die.'

She looked upon Aurelius, saying, 'Is this really true? I never understood you till now. But, by God who gave me my soul and my life, I will never in word or deed be faithless to my husband.' Then, trying to make light of it, she added, 'This is my final word, Aurelius: on the day when you have removed all the rocks, stone by stone, from end to end of Brittany, so that they shall be no more a peril to ship or boat – I say, when you have made those coasts so clean of rocks that there is not a pebble to be seen, I will grant you my love, and love you better than any other man, I swear it!'

'Is there no more grace in you than this?' said he.

'No, by the Lord who made me,' said she. 'I know well that I have asked what cannot be done. So let this madness pass out of your heart.'

'Madam,' groaned Aurelius, 'that is impossible.' And with that word, he left her.

Her friends now came about her, and they roamed among the alleys, and began anew their revels, and at nightfall went joyously home. Only the wretched Aurelius, alas! went home with a heavy heart, and, almost out of his wits, he fell upon his knees, lifted his hands to heaven, and prayed: 'Apollo, god and governor of plants, herbs, trees, and flowers, cast your merciful eye on the wretched Aurelius! and bid your bright sister Lucina, queen of the sea, to help you. You know, lord, how she is quickened and lighted by your fire, and follows your will as the tides follow hers. Wherefore I pray of you a miracle, O Phoebus! Let her bring about so great a flood, that it shall o'ertop the highest rock in Brittany by five fathoms, and let this flood last two years. Then may I surely say to my lady: Your behest is done, the rocks are gone. Lord Phoebus, do this miracle for me, behold the tears on my cheek, and have pity on my pain!' So saying, he fell down in a swoon, and lay long in a trance. His brother, who knew his grief, took him up and bore him to bed, not knowing whether he would live or die.

And now the flower of chivalry, Arviragus, is come home again in glory. O now thou art blissful, Dorigen, with thy husband in thy arms! All was dancing, and feasting, and making good cheer.

But sweet Aurelius lay two years in anguish and torment, and got no comfort all this time of any save his brother, who was a scholar. He grieved in private over his brother's trouble; till at last he remembered a book dealing with natural magic, which he had seen when he was a student in Orleans in France. His fellow-student, a bachelor of law, had left the book upon his desk, and being curious he had looked into it, and read much about the strange operations of the mansions of the moon, and other crazy things, which nowadays we should not value at a fly. But, remembering this book, his heart danced for joy, and he said to himself, 'Here lies my brother's cure! for I am sure there are sciences by which men can work wonders and apparitions. Now if I could find in Orleans some old fellow who has studied the moon and other natural magic, he should easily help my brother to his love; such a magician could make the rocks of Brittany appear to disappear for a

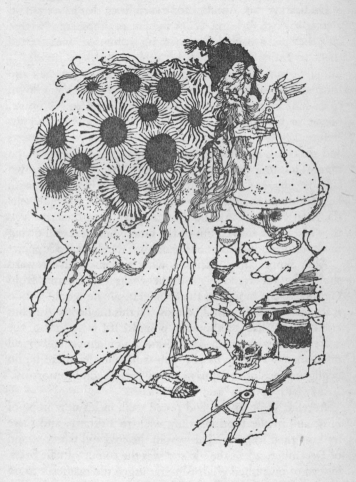

year or two; and then the lady must either keep her word, or be shamed for ever.'

On hearing this, Aurelius took such heart that he started up at once to go to Orleans. When they were almost come to that city, they met a young clerk roaming by himself, who greeted them in Latin; after which he amazed them by saying, 'I know the cause of your coming.' And before they went a step further, he told them all their purpose. Aurelius sprang down from his horse, and went with the magician to his house. Never in his life had he seen such luxury and splendour. Before they went to supper, the magician showed him forests and parks full of wild deer, and falcons slaying herons, and knights jousting on a plain, and last he showed him his own lady dancing, and Aurelius himself seemed to be dancing with her. Suddenly the magician clapped his hands, and farewell! the revel vanished. All the time they had seen these marvels they had never moved out of the house, but were still sitting in his study among his books. And then they went to supper.

After supper they discussed what the magician's reward should be for removing all the rocks of Brittany from Gironde to the mouth of the Seine. He said he would not do it for less than a thousand pounds. To this the happy Aurelius cried out, 'What is a thousand pounds? If I were lord of the wide world, which men say is round, I would give it all to seal our bargain. I swear to pay you truly; but let there be no negligence or sloth – let us not tarry here beyond tomorrow.'

'My faith upon it,' said the magician.

Aurelius went to bed and rested well, in his new hope of bliss; and in the morning they went to Brittany, and there took up their lodging. This was in the cold and frosty season of December, when the old sun was the colour of pale brass, instead of burnished gold. Aurelius urged the magician to do at once the work which should end his pain. The subtle clerk bade him be patient till the time was right for juggleries and illusions, by which he should make it appear that the rocks of Brittany had vanished; and at last, according to astrology of which I know nothing, the time arrived for him to put into practice his wretched tricks and superstitions. Then, by means of his astronomical tables, his charts, his compasses, his roots, proportions and equations, he calculated which of the moon's mansions was favourable to his operations, and without further delay worked such a spell, that all the rocks appeared to vanish from man's sight.

Aurelius, now hoping, now despairing, had waited night and day for the accomplishment of the miracle. When he knew the obstacle to his wishes was removed, he fell down at his master's feet and thanked him in the name of Venus. Then he made his way back to the temple where he knew he would find his lady; and in due time saluted her with a trembling heart. 'My sovereign lady,' said this unhappy man, 'whom I fear and love with all my might, and would displease least of any in this world, did I not love you so that I could die at your feet: O madam, you remember what you promised. I claim nothing of you but your grace, and your remembrance of what you said to me once in a garden; heaven knows you said it, unworthy though I am. Madam, as much for your honour's sake as to save my life, I come to tell you that I have done what you commanded; go see for yourself, and then say whether I am to live or die. For the rocks of Brittany have vanished.'

Then he left her, and she stood stunned and white of face; she had never dreamed of being caught in such a trap.

'Alas!' said she, 'that this should ever happen. I never thought such a monstrous marvel possible; it is against the law of nature.' And she went home sorrowfully, and wept for two days. Arviragus was absent at the time, and she told no one of her distress, but, moaning and often swooning, determined that rather than leave her husband she would kill herself. On the third night Arviragus returned, and found her weeping; and when he asked her why, she wept more bitterly still.

'Alas, that ever I was born!' said she. 'Hear what I am sworn to do.' And she told him all you know already.

Her husband, looking tenderly at her, said, 'Is this all, Dorigen?'

'All?' said she. 'Though it be God's will, it is too much.'

'Wife,' said he, 'you must keep your word. God pardon me, my love for you is so great, that I had rather suffer than that you should break your troth. His troth is the greatest thing man has to keep.' Then he wept, and said, 'On pain of death, I bid you tell this to no one as long as you live. I will endure my hurt as best I can; and you must not even look sad, lest folk should guess anything.' Then he called a squire and a maid. 'Go with Dorigen,' he said, 'and escort her to such-and-such a place.' And they went forth with her, not knowing why she went.

It chanced that the loving Aurelius met her in the street on her way to the garden where she had given him her promise; for he too was on his way there. He greeted her joyously, and asked her where she was going; and she answered, as though she were half-mad, 'To the garden, as my husband bids me, to keep my troth, alas, alas!'

Aurelius began to ponder, and his heart ached for her and her sorrow, and for Arviragus the noble knight, who had bade her keep her promise. He was so torn with pity that he knew he had rather lose his love than do an ill thing against such goodness and generosity. So he said simply to her:

'Madam, tell your lord Arviragus that, because of your distress, and because of his great gentleness, which would rather suffer shame (and that were a pity) than you should break your troth: I myself would rather suffer for ever, than part the love between you two. I release you, madam, from every bond and oath you ever made me, and I plight my troth never to ask anything of you again, and so I take my leave of the best and truest wife I ever knew. For a squire can do a gentle deed, as well as a knight.'

She thanked him on her knees, and went home to her husband and told him all; and it is impossible for me to describe his joy. What need to speak more of Arviragus and his wife Dorigen? They lived their lives in utter bliss, there was never any anger between them, he cherished her as though she were a queen, and she was true to him for ever-more. You get no more of me about these two.

But Aurelius, left forlorn, cursed the day he was born. 'Alas!' said he. 'How shall I pay the magician? What shall I do? I must sell my heritage, and go forth a beggar, for I cannot stay here to shame my kindred with my poverty. But first I will go to him and see whether he will let me pay him a little, year by year. He may do me this grace; but whether or no, I will keep my troth with him.'

With a heavy heart he took from his coffers five hundred pounds in gold, and brought them to the magician, and be-seeched him to allow him time to pay the rest, saying, 'Master, I can boast that I never yet failed in my troth; I will pay my debt to you though it leaves me a beggar in nothing but my shirt. But if you will take my surety and grant me a respite of two or three years, I need not sell my heritage.'

The magician heard him out, and answered gravely, 'Have I not kept my bargain with you?'

'Yes, well and truly,' said he.

'Have you not had your lady?'

'No, no,' he said sorrowfully.

'Why not? Tell me.'

So Aurelius told him what you already know. He told how Arviragus was so noble that he would rather die of sorrow than that his wife should be false to her word; and he told of

Dorigen's distress, and how she would rather die than leave her husband; and that she had given her troth in innocence, knowing nothing of the powers of magic. 'That filled me with such pity for her, that as freely as her husband sent her to me, I sent her back to him. There is no more to say.'

The magician then said, 'Dear brother, each of you has done nobly by the other; you are a squire, and he is a knight, and God forbid that clerk cannot do a noble thing as well as either of you. Sir, I release you from your thousand pounds, as freely as though we had never known each other; and I will not take a single penny from you for my wisdom or my work. You paid for my keep, and that is enough, and so farewell and good day.' And he got on his horse and went his way.

My lords, I would ask you this question: which of them was the noblest? My tale is ended.

PART THREE
Magicians of Folklore

The Magician's Horse

THERE was once a Prince, the youngest son of a King, who set out to seek his fortune – for there was none to be found in his own land. After many adventures that brought him no fortune at all, he found himself lost in a mighty forest where he lived for several days on roots and berries.

At last, on the morning of the fifth day he came, weak with starvation, to a palace standing in a clearing planted with gardens.

The Prince walked through the garden and into the court-yard of the palace: but he saw nobody. He walked into the palace itself and passed from room to room, each shining with treasures of tapestry and furniture, ornaments and pictures, all swept and dusted and as shining as the polished marble and cedar of the floors – but still there was no sign of any living creature.

At last he came to the dining hall and saw there a table spread with dainty dishes, steaming hot and freshly cooked; with bowls of fresh fruit, and with flagons of choice wines. Then, because his hunger was so great, and there was no one to bid him eat or to say him nay, the Prince sat down at the table and ate and drank until he was satisfied.

As soon as he had finished his meal, all that was left of it, with the dishes and the glasses, vanished silently away leaving only the bare table.

This struck the Prince as strange, and he became more and more convinced that the whole palace was the work of en-chantment.

So once more he set out in search of any inhabitants; and as evening was beginning to fall he met suddenly with an old man in a long black robe and a strangely shaped hat, who advanced towards him and said:

'Young man, what are you doing wandering about my castle and helping yourself to my dinner?'

To which the Prince replied, bowing low: 'Reverend Sir, forgive me. I lost my way in the forest and was dying of hunger when I chanced to find your castle. There was no one here, and seeing the meal set out I made so bold as to eat of it. Now I am ready to serve you faithfully if you will make me your servant – unless you have invisible servants to do your will by magic, and do not need me.'

'Very well,' said the old man, who was in fact a very powerful Magician, 'I'll employ you. There are many things that can be done better by an ordinary servant than by any of the spells at my command. So now your duty will be to fetch wood from the forest each morning to keep the great stove in my tower always burning brightly. And besides that you will have charge of the great black horse in my stable – both to feed and groom him night and morning. If you do this you shall eat and drink and sleep softly, and I will pay you a florin a day.'

So the Prince became the Magician's servant, and worked well and faithfully for some time. One day, however, he forgot to make up the fire in the stove, and it was almost out when the Magician came storming into the room below the tower and cried:

'Make up the stove, you dolt! If it goes out, half my magic will grow cold and be lost to me!'

So the Prince made haste to coax the fire back into life, and soon the stove was roaring away merrily.

'Now do not let this happen again,' said the Magician, 'or be sure I shall punish you cruelly.'

And after this the Prince's life was by no means so pleasant; for not only did the Magician keep a sharp eye on him, and never hesitate to strike him for the smallest fault, but the

Prince began to realize that his master was preparing some great magic up in the tower above the room where the stove stood – and he knew that this magic was evil and would bring misery to many.

One day as the Prince sat brooding sadly in a corner of the stable, the black horse spoke to him suddenly:

'Prince, come into my stall and listen carefully to what I say.'

The Prince was greatly surprised to hear the horse speak, but nothing seemed impossible in the Magician's castle, and so he made haste to do as he was told.

'Listen carefully,' said the Horse in a low voice. 'Our master is, as you know, a wicked magician and both of us are anxious to escape from him. As it happens I myself am a bit of a magician among horses, though of white magic, in spite of my colour. Now, if you will trust me absolutely I'll help you to escape, to overcome the Magician who holds us – and to make your fortune into the bargain.'

'I perceive, my good friend, that you are a horse of honour,' said the Prince. 'Therefore tell me what to do and I will obey your every command.'

'Good,' said the Horse. 'Fetch the bridle and saddle from that cupboard and fasten them upon me. Take the bottle which is beside them: it contains an ointment that will make your hair shine like pure gold. Then put all the wood that you can gather together on to the stove until the flames roar up to the ceiling.'

The Prince did all that the Horse told him. He put on the saddle and bridle; he rubbed the ointment into his hair until it shone like gold; and he made such a big fire in the stove that soon the flames reached up to the ceiling which, being made of wood, presently caught fire so that before long, the flames roared up the tower as if it had been a chimney, and the whole castle was burning.

Then he hurried back to the stable and the Horse said to him: 'There is one thing more. Hurry before we are caught by the fire. In the cupboard you will find a looking-glass, a brush and a riding-whip. Bring them with you, mount on my back, and ride as hard as you can, for now the castle is burning merrily.'

The Prince did as the Horse bade him. Scarcely was he mounted when the Horse was off and away through the forest at break-neck speed.

But they had scarcely left the gardens when the Magician returned – just in time to see his castle crash to the ground in flames. Taking his magic crystal from his pouch he gazed swiftly into it and saw his servant riding away on the black horse.

'That evil beast has betrayed me!' he cried. So saying he sprang upon the roan horse which was his usual mount, and galloped in pursuit.

As the Prince rode the quick ears of his steed heard the sound of pursuing feet. 'Look behind you,' he said, 'and see if the Magician is following.'

The Prince turned in his saddle and saw a cloud like smoke or dust in the distance.

'We must hurry,' said the Horse, and sped on.

When they had galloped for some time more, the Horse asked again: 'Look behind and see how near the Wizard is.'

'He is quite close now,' replied the Prince.

'Then throw the looking-glass on the ground,' said the Horse.

So the Prince threw it; and when the Magician came up the roan horse stepped on the mirror and it crushed to pieces beneath his feet. The sharp glass cut the iron shoes from his hooves, so that he stumbled and went lame.

So there was nothing for it but for the Magician to return to the ruins of his castle for fresh shoes. And when he had shod the roan horse he set off once more after the Black Horse – for he felt that he must recapture it or else his magic would be of no avail.

In the meanwhile the Prince had gone a great distance. But presently the quick ears of the Black Horse caught from afar the sound of following feet.

'Dismount and put your ear to the ground,' he said. 'And tell me what you hear.'

The Prince did so, and at once exclaimed: 'I feel the earth trembling; there is a sound like distant thunder. The Magician cannot be far behind.'

'Mount at once,' shouted the Black Horse, 'and I will gallop my fastest.' And off he went so fast that the earth seemed to fly from under his hooves.

'Look back once more,' he said after a short time, 'and tell me what you see.'

'I see a cloud and a flame,' answered the Prince. 'But it is still a long way off.'

'We must make haste indeed,' said the Black Horse. But very soon he asked again: 'Look back and tell me what you see. He cannot be far off.'

'He is close behind us,' cried the Prince. 'His great roan horse is breathing smoke and fire out of his nostrils, and very soon flames will be burning us!'

'Then throw down the brush on the ground in front of them!' said the Black Horse.

The Prince flung it down immediately; and in an instant the bristles of the brush grew up into such a thick wood, twined with brambles and creepers that even a bird could not have got through it. And there was nothing for it but for the Magician to return to the ruins of his castle as fast as the roan horse would carry him to fetch an axe and return with it to cut his way through the wood.

This took him some time, and the Prince and the Black

Horse had got well ahead. But presently they again heard the sound of pursuing feet. 'Look back!' neighed the Black Horse. 'Look back, and tell me if he is following!'

'Yes,' answered the Prince. 'I hear the thunder of the roan horse's hooves and see a cloud of smoke in the distance.'

'Let us hurry on,' said the Black Horse, and he seemed to fly over the ground. But before long the rumble of thunder drew closer and closer behind them, and he said: 'Look back once more and see how close he is.'

'He is just behind us,' answered the Prince. 'The flames are pouring from the roan horse's nostrils and you will soon feel them burning your flanks.'

'Then you must throw down the whip between him and us!' cried the Black Horse. The Prince did so, and in the twinkling of an eye the whip was changed into a broad river. Into the water went the roan horse with the Magician on his back, and in a moment they were covered by the swift-flowing stream, and the fire was put out that had flamed from the roan horse's nostrils, and with it all the black magic of the Magician.

'Now we may rest,' said the Black Horse, 'for there is nothing else to fear. The wicked Magician is dead and all his spells are broken. Neither he nor the wicked roan who served him could survive the pure running water of the river. But now it remains for you to win the fortune which you set out to seek. Do as I bid you, and I will not leave you until your fortune is won: for without your help I could never have escaped from the Magician or brought him and his familiar to the end they deserved.'

'My kind friend, I will do anything you tell me,' answered the Prince.

'Then go to the riverside and cut the willow wand you will find there,' said the Black Horse. And when the Prince returned with the wand, the Horse continued: 'Strike the ground three times with the wand and you will see a door at your feet.'

The Prince did as he was bidden, and at once the earth opened in front of him revealing a steep ramp leading down to a door behind which he found a large vaulted stone hall.

'Lead me down into the hall and leave me there,' said the Black Horse. 'I will remain in it until you need me. For you must go through the fields until you reach a garden in the midst of which is a King's palace. When you get there you must ask to be taken into the King's service. Farewell – and do not forget me.'

So the Prince led the Horse down into the vault; and when he had tied a scarf round his head like a turban so as to conceal his golden hair, he went to the palace which was no more than a league away, and obtained the post of under-gardener in the King's gardens. For with his hair hidden, and dressed in the rough garments which the Magician had given him when his own wore out, no one could tell that he was really a Prince.

'You shall have a florin a day, a horse to help you carry the leaves and rubbish away, and as much food and drink as you need,' said the head gardener. And the Prince agreed to this. But each night when his day's work was ended and he had eaten half his supper in the toolshed at the end of the garden, which had become his home, he would walk the league to the cave and give the other half of his supper to the Magician's Horse.

One evening when he went to the cave, the Horse said to him: 'My faithful friend, the time is coming when I may reward you for all you have done for me. Tomorrow many lords and ladies will be coming to the Palace where the three daughters of the King are to have husbands chosen for them. They will all meet on the terrace, and each Princess will toss a golden apple into the air, and he at whose feet it comes to rest will be her husband, whoever he may be. You must make certain that you are working in the garden at the foot of the steps leading down from the terrace, under the white rose tree which grows there.'

The Prince did just as the Magician's Horse had told him. And when the third and by far the most beautiful of the Princesses tossed her golden apple into the air, it rolled across the terrace, down the steps, and came to rest at the feet of the disguised Prince who was busily brushing up the leaves under the white rose tree.

The Princess ran after the apple, and as the Prince stooped to pick it up, the scarf slipped for a moment from his head, and she saw his glorious golden hair framing his handsome face – and loved him on the instant.

But the King was very sad, for his youngest daughter was the one whom he loved best. However there was no help for it, since he had given his royal word. So next day there was a triple wedding, and when the elder Princesses were married to Princes in splendid robes, the youngest Princess married the garden boy and went to live with him in the toolshed at the end of the garden

Not long after this a great army came marching towards the border of the Kingdom, meaning to conquer it and make all the people into slaves.

The King gathered his own army and set out to do battle with the invaders, and the Princes who had married his two elder daughters went with him mounted on stately steeds and clad in shining armour. But the husband of the youngest Princess had nothing but the old broken-down horse which helped him in his garden work; and the King, who was ashamed of this son-in-law, refused to give him any other.

The Prince, however, was determined not to be left behind. So he went into the garden, mounted the sorry nag, and set out to join the King's army. But he had not ridden more than a mile before the old horse stumbled and fell, and it was obvious that it could not go any further.

In despair the Prince ran across the fields to the vault where the Magician's Horse still lived. And as soon as he entered the Horse said to him:

'I was waiting for you. Saddle and bridle me, and then go into the next room where you will find a suit of armour and a sword. Put on the armour and we will ride forth together to battle.'

The Prince did as he was told; and when he had mounted his magic steed his armour glittered in the sun, and his hair gleamed like molten gold, and altogether he looked so brave and noble and handsome that no one would have recognized him as the under-gardener who swept up the dead leaves on the Palace lawns and paths.

The Magician's Horse bore him away at a great pace, and when they reached the battlefield they found that the King was losing; many of his men had been slain, and the barbarian invaders seemed just about to turn the retreating army into a rout and sweep into the capital city to bring ruin and havoc.

But when the Warrior Prince on his great black charger, in his glittering armour, appeared on the field, hewing right and left with his sword, the enemy were terrified, and very soon fled in all directions, leaving the King master of the day.

When the battle was over and the remnants of the barbarians fleeing for their lives, the King turned back to thank the Warrior Prince who had saved the day and freed the country from the threat of bondage and destruction.

The Prince had one slight wound in the leg, and the King knelt down and bandaged it with his own cambric handkerchief embroidered with a crown and the royal arms.

'Royal sir,' said the King, 'I have commanded a litter to be brought in which to convey you back to our city to receive thanks of all our people for preserving us from slavery this day.'

But the Prince begged rather to be helped on to his own black steed; and as soon as he was in the saddle the Magician's Horse rose suddenly into the air and bore him out of sight, while the soldiers cried: 'A god and no mortal man has come to our rescue!'

And throughout all the land all the people began to say among themselves: 'Who can the hero be who has saved us in the hour of our greatest need? He cannot be a mere mortal – surely he must be a god!'

And the King said: 'If only I could find him, and if he proves to be a man and no god, I would give him even up to the half of my kingdom.'

But the Prince had returned home to the humble toolshed where he lived, after doffing his armour, donning the scarf round his golden hair, and thanking the Magician's Horse for what he had done for him that day. He was so weary when he reached the toolshed that he flung himself down immediately on his bed and fell into a deep sleep.

His wife, the Princess, bent over him – and noticed suddenly that a handkerchief was bound about his wounded leg. She examined it closely, and in amazement recognized it by the crown and the coat-of-arms as belonging to her father.

So she ran straight to the Palace and told the King what she had found. And he and his other two sons-in-law followed her back to the toolshed, and saw her husband the under-gardener lying asleep on the bed. But the scarf, which he always wore about his head, was hanging loose, and the Princess was easily

able to pull it off without waking her husband. Then his golden hair gleamed on the pillow, and they all recognized him as the hero who had fought and won the great battle for them.

After this, there was no hiding the truth any longer. The whole country broke out into wild rejoicings; the King rewarded his warrior son-in-law with half the kingdom, and the Prince and Princess reigned happily over it.

As for the Magician's Horse, the Prince lost no time in hastening to the vaulted stable where he lived. But he had not stayed to be thanked: as soon as he had paid his debt of friendship and gratitude to the Prince, he had flown away to his own land where he was in truth King over all the Horses, and in his own right a Master Magician of the best and finest sort.

The Gifts of the Magician

ONCE upon a time there was a boy who lived with his father in the middle of a forest. Near their hut was a grove of trees in which the black-game made their nests, and the old man often warned his son against shooting any of these birds.

But one day when the boy was almost grown up, and his father was away from home, he could withstand the temptation no longer. Taking his bow and arrows, the youth got ready for the evening flight, and shot a black-cock just as it was flying towards its nest.

He had aimed badly, however, and the bird was only wounded. For when he went to pick it up, it fluttered away along the ground. He ran after it, as it did not seem as if it would be difficult to catch; but it always managed just to elude him, and it led him far away into the heart of the forest. Presently it began to grow dark, and the young man felt that it would be foolish to go any further in case night should overtake him before he could reach home. He thought it would be easy to retrace his steps; but very soon he found that he was completely lost.

After a while he decided that he must seek shelter for the night; for he had heard that there were wolves deep in the lesser-known parts of the forest, and anyhow it was getting very cold. So he set off briskly in as straight a line as he could keep.

Soon, however, night fell, and he began to hesitate and feel afraid. The full moon rising presently gave him more light, and he had just come out into an open forest glade, when he heard the hunting cry of a wolf-pack, and saw a Magician come running towards him with the wolves close behind.

The youth immediately set an arrow to his bow and shot it

through the heart of the leader of the pack. A few more well-aimed arrows sent the rest of the wolves scurrying away in terror, and the youth turned to the Magician, who said:

'I thank you indeed, young man, for you have saved my life. These evil beasts came upon me suddenly when I had never a charm nor a spell nor any magic implement with me – and with all my knowledge of magic there was nothing I could do to prevent them from tearing me to pieces. But come with me now to my dwelling and I will reward you worthily.'

'Indeed,' said the young man, 'at the moment all I ask is shelter for the night! I have been wandering all day in the forest unable to find my way home.'

'Then come with me. You must be hungry as well as tired,' said the Magician, and led the way to his house where the young man had a splendid supper and thereafter fell into a deep sleep.

Early next morning the Magician left the house, telling his one attendant to have the midday meal ready when he returned.

Now the Magician's housekeeper was very jealous, and she was afraid that the Magician would heap great rewards on the young man. So later in the morning she went to wake him, meaning to tell him that the Magician was going to cast him under some terrible spell, and that she would help him to escape.

But the Magician had cast him into a charmed sleep and nothing she could do was able to wake him for more than a moment, to open his eyes, shut them again quickly and sink into even deeper sleep.

So she was forced to leave him and prepare the food for the midday meal. Just before the Magician returned for this, the charmed sleep fell suddenly from the young man and he got up, dressed and came down into the room where the housekeeper was setting out the meal.

The Magician arrived at almost the same moment, but before he came into the room she just had time to whisper to the young man:

'If he offers you a reward, ask for the horse which stands in the third stall in his stable.'

This she did feeling sure that, rather than give up so valuable and magical a possession, the Magician would silence for ever the man who had been so foolish as to ask for it.

When the meal was ended the Magician said: 'And now, my young friend and preserver, you must be on your way. But first of all tell me what you will have from me as a reward for your courage.'

'Give me the horse which stands in the third stall of your stable,' answered the young man. 'I have a long way to go before I get home – and I have taken a fancy to that horse.'

'It is the best horse in my stable,' said the Magician. 'I beg you to ask for something else.'

'No, that is what I have set my heart on,' replied the young man.

For a long time the Magician sat in silence. Then suddenly he smiled and said: 'You shall have the horse: though it may not stay with you for all its life. And I will also give you a zither, a fiddle and a flute. If you are in danger, touch the strings of the zither; and if no one comes to your aid, then play on the fiddle; but if that brings no help, blow on the flute.'

The young man thanked the Magician, and fastening his treasures to the saddle, mounted the horse and rode off. He had not gone many miles when, to his great surprise, the horse remarked suddenly:

'It's very foolish of you to go home just now. Your father will only beat you for shooting the black-cock. Why not let me take you to the city where the King lives and see if we cannot make your fortune?'

'I've no objection to that,' said the young man. 'Therefore go where you will and I will let the reins lie loose on your neck.'

So they went through the forest and out into the land beyond until they came to the city. And there the horse was admired so much that the King came to hear of him and sent for the young man to ask him to sell the horse for any price he cared to ask.

'Do not sell me,' whispered the horse, 'but ask the King to take me into his stables, and to make you his Master of Horse. And tell him that if he does so, the other horses will catch my beauty and all grow as beautiful as I am.'

The King readily agreed to this; and sure enough within a year every horse in the Royal Stables was as beautiful as the Magician's Horse – even the oldest and most decrepit grew young and strong and sleek once more.

All this delighted the King, and his new Master of Horse was treated as one of the most honoured of all his Courtiers.

But the old groom who had looked after the royal horses before the young man arrived – and had made plenty of money in secret by selling the grain on which they were supposed to feed, and by other means known to wicked and unscrupulous grooms – was eaten up with jealousy and hate. And he very soon began to plot against his rival, and carry false, lying tales about him to the King.

For a long time he had no success. But at last one day he hit upon a scheme which he felt sure would get rid of his rival once and for all. So he went to the King and said:

'Your Majesty, the young Master of the Horse has been boasting that he can find your famous war-horse which was lost in the forest as you returned from the wars two years ago.'

Now the King had never ceased to mourn for this his favourite horse – and in those days the man who had the best war-horse was the man who had the best engine of war – and he sent at once for his Master of the Horse in a state of great excitement, and cried:

'Find my war-horse and bring him back to me in three days, as you have said that you could do – or I will have you torn to pieces by horses as a liar and a boaster.'

The young man was horrified at this command, but he bowed before the King – and then hurried off to the stable to consult the Magician's horse.

'Do not worry,' said the horse placidly. 'Ask the King for the flesh of three oxen cut up into small pieces; put it in bags and hang them on my saddle, and ride forth upon me with a loose bridle until we come to a certain river which I know. Soon a horse will come up out of the water – but take no notice of it. A second horse will come up, but ignore that also. But when a third horse comes up, throw my bridle over it, and lead it back to the King.'

All happened as the Magician's horse had said. But as soon as they started for home with the war-horse following them, the Magician's horse said:

'The Magician's raven will be upon us in a minute and will try to devour us both. But throw it the pieces of the oxen's flesh handful by handful, and I will gallop like the wind, and soon we shall be out of his clutches.'

The young man did as he was told, and so escaped from the Magician's raven, who was as big as a young dragon, and so brought the war-horse safely back to the King.

The old groom was even more jealous of the Master of the Horse after this, and far more determined to bring about his downfall. Presently he thought of another scheme, and went to the King and said:

'Your Majesty, the young Master of the Horse has been boasting again. This time he says that he can find the young Queen who is lost as easily as he found your war-horse.'

Now the King had taken a young Princess, against her will,

to be his Queen, and she had vanished away as he led her from the church after the marriage ceremony. He was madly in love with her and as soon as he heard the groom's words, he sent for the young man and cried:

'Bring me back my wife, as you say you can do, within three days – or wild horses shall devour you to satisfy their hunger.'

The poor young man was filled with horror at these words, but he only bowed to the King – and went in haste to consult his friend in the stable.

'Nothing easier,' said the Magician's horse. 'You have only to lead me to the same river that we visited yesterday, and I will plunge into it and take my proper shape again. For I am the King's wife, who was turned into a horse by the Magician: but whether to save me from the King or to have me for himself I do not know.'

The young man did as he was told. And as soon as the horse had disappeared beneath the waters of the river there arose from the same spot a young woman so lovely that the young man fell in love with her there and then.

However he led her back to the King; only to find that his enemy the groom had been stirring up more trouble for him and had made the King believe that he was the leader of a revolution to murder him and make himself King in his stead.

'Take him to the gallows at once!' cried the King, and the wretched young man was led away. But when he mounted the scaffold he remembered a custom of that country, and said:

'Bring me my zither and let me play a farewell tune upon it. You cannot refuse me: it is my last request.'

So the zither which the Magician had given him was brought, and the young man passed his fingers gently over the strings. Scarcely had the first notes sounded than the hangman and his assistant executioner began to dance, and the louder the music grew the higher they capered, till at last they cried for mercy. But the young man paid no heed, and went on playing until they sank to the ground utterly exhausted, and declared that the hanging must be put off until tomorrow – for they could not stir a finger to do it.

In a great fury the King hastened to the scaffold with all his Court, and two new hangmen.

'Let me but play my funeral dirge on my fiddle,' said the young man; and the King could not refuse him. But as soon as the bow touched the strings the leg of every man there was lifted high, and they danced to the sound of the music, King, Courtiers and all, until the sun was sinking in the west and not one of them could stand on his feet any longer.

Next day the King and Court and a huge crowd assembled once more to see the young man hanged. And once more he made his last request, as the law allowed.

'Let me but play one tune on my flute, and I shall die happy.'

'No, no!' cried the King. 'Your infernal fiddling had me dancing yesterday until I could not move a limb. I have slept like a log from then until now – and now I am so stiff that I can hardly move.'

But the young man insisted on his rights, and the people all murmured that the law could not be broken, so that the King was forced to agree, and the flute was brought.

Before the young man began to play, the King had himself bound securely to a large oak tree which stood near by, so that he could not be made to dance again.

Then the young man began to play on his flute, and the King found his body moving to the sound until his clothes were in tatters from the hard bark of the tree, and the skin was nearly rubbed off his back.

Suddenly the young man played a louder note than usual and the Magician appeared in a flash of light.

'My young friend,' he said, 'you have sent for me. What danger are you in?'

'They want to hang me on the false accusations of the groom,' was the answer. 'See, the gallows is all ready and the hangman is only waiting for me to stop playing before he strings me up.'

'Oh, I will put that right!' said the Magician. And with that he spoke a Word of Power and blew towards the gallows – and on the instant it flew away through the air, and no one could tell where it came down.

'And who was it ordered you to be hanged?' asked the Magician.

The young man pointed to the King, who was still bound to the oak tree. And without wasting words the Magician spoke another Word of Power and blew once more: and both the King and the oak tree soared into the air and went spinning off out of sight – and no one knows to this day if they have yet fallen to the earth again.

After this the young man married the Queen and became King of the country, to the great delight of all the people. This was too much for the jealous groom, and he died there and then of envy.

But the Magician, having seen his young friend happily married and the popular King of a mighty country, felt that he had paid his debt to the full. So he wiped his hands, spoke a Word of Power, and returned to his own house in the middle of the forest.

The Magician's Pupil

THERE was once a man who had a son who was very clever at reading, and delighted in doing so, and could remember everything that he read. When he was old enough he set out into the wide world to seek his fortune, and he decided that the first thing to do was to go into service.

As he was walking through the forest he met a tall old man with horn-rimmed spectacles and a long staff whom he realized at once must be a Magician.

'Where are you going?' asked the Magician.

'I am going about seeking for service,' answered the boy.

'Will you serve me?' asked the Magician.

'I will indeed,' said the boy. 'I was ready to accept the first offer: just as well you as anyone else.'

'But can you read?' asked the Magician.

'As well as if I were a priest or a schoolmaster,' answered the boy.

'Then you are no use to me,' said the Magician. 'In fact I want a boy who can't read at all. His only work will be to dust my old books.'

So the Magician went on his way, and left the boy looking sadly after him.

'What a pity I didn't get that place with the old Magician,' thought the boy. 'It was just the very thing for me ... I wonder now ... He looked as if he was very short-sighted, and he is certain to be very absent-minded: all clever scholars and magicians are. Yes, I'll try it!'

With this he took off his jacket and put it on inside out, brushed back his hair which had been hanging over his eyes, and set off running his hardest through the wood. When he judged he had gone far enough, he came out on to the road and set off along it in the direction from which he had come.

In a few minutes he met the Magician, who had continued on his way deep in thought.

'Where are you going, my boy?' asked the Magician, not recognizing him in the least.

'Oh, I'm looking for a job,' said the boy. 'I'm quite old enough to earn my own living.'

'Will you come and work for me?' asked the Magician.

'I'd be delighted to do so,' answered the boy, 'if it's a job I can do, and the pay is good enough.'

'But can you read?' asked the Magician anxiously.

'Not a word,' answered the boy blithely.

'Then you're just the lad I want,' cried the Magician. 'Come along with me, and you shall have good food and plenty of it, and I will pay you a shilling a week.'

So the boy took service with the Magician, and as he had nothing to do but dust his master's books, he found plenty of time to read them as well, until at last he was just as learned as his master and knew just as many magic spells and could perform all kinds of magic – including being able to change himself into the shape of any animal or any other thing that he pleased.

As soon as he had learned all this the boy decided that there was no point in remaining in the Magician's service. So he ran away and returned home to his parents.

Next time there was a market in the neighbouring town he told his parents about the magic he had learnt, and said:

'Tomorrow I shall change myself into a magnificent horse, and father can take me to the market and sell me. There is no need to worry. I shall come home safe and sound in my own form.'

So next day the boy changed himself into a horse and his father led the animal to the market which was being held in the town. It was such a fine horse that it sold for a great sum

of money. And when the bargain had been made and the money paid, the purchaser led the horse away. But as soon as they got out of the town, the boy changed back into his own shape when no one was looking, and went home.

The story of the magnificent horse which had been bought in the market and had disappeared so mysteriously, spread all over the countryside, and at last the Magician heard of it.

'Aha!' said he. 'This must be that boy of mine who be-fooled me, and ran away. I must catch him quickly and deal with him – for he seems to have learnt my best magic, and will be a danger to me.'

The next time there was a market the boy again changed himself into a horse and was taken and sold for a fine price by his father. But the Magician was on the watch, and as soon as he saw the horse he realized that it was no ordinary animal but must be the boy in that shape, transformed by enchantment. So he went into the inn where the bargain was being sealed with a drink, and offered so much more for the horse that at last he managed to buy it from the purchaser.

As soon as the Magician was the owner of the enchanted horse, he led it straight to the nearest smithy, and instructed the smith to prepare a red-hot nail to drive into its mouth, because once that was done it could never again change its shape.

When the boy realized what the Magician was about to do, he immediately changed himself into a dove, and flew up into the air. The Magician at once changed himself into a hawk and flew after it. The dove at once changed itself into a gold ring and fell into a girl's lap.

The hawk then turned into a handsome young man and offered the girl a great sum of money for the gold ring, but she would not part with it, since she thought that it had fallen down to her from Heaven. However the Magician kept on offering her more and more for it, until at last the boy grew frightened, and the gold ring changed suddenly into a grain of barley, and fell to the ground. The Magician in an instant turned into a hen and began to search desperately for the grain to gobble it up; but the boy turned from a grain of barley into a pole-cat, and bit off the hen's head with a single snap.

The Magician was now dead and done for, and the pole-cat returned to his human form and told the whole story to the girl. And she was so impressed by what she heard that she promptly agreed to marry the boy, and they lived happily ever after and had no need to use the Magician's charms any further.

The Magician who Had no Heart

ONCE upon a time there were seven brothers who were orphans and had no sister. So they were obliged to do all the housework themselves, and they did not like this at all. The only thing to do was to get married, and so they decided that six of them should set out to seek for brides, while the youngest remained at home to look after the house. But they promised to bring back the prettiest girl they could find to be his wife.

As the six young men went on their way through the wide world they came to a little house in the forest where lived an old, old Magician with a long white beard.

'Greetings, brave young men!' cried the Magician in a high cracked voice. 'Whither away so fast and so cheerily?'

'We are going through the wide world to seek brides for ourselves, and the prettiest one for our youngest brother whom we have left at home,' they replied.

'Oh, my dear young men!' said the Magician. 'I am so lonely here. Pray bring me a bride as well, the youngest and prettiest you can find!'

'What does a shrivelled old thing like that want with a pretty young bride?' said the brothers to each other. And they went on their way laughing at the old grey man in the wood, until they came to a near-by town.

Here they were lucky enough to find seven sisters, as young and as lovely as anyone could wish to see, and all eager to find husbands. So what more natural than that each brother should choose one of the sisters to be his bride, and take the youngest and prettiest with them to be the wife of their brother at home.

On their return journey they came again to the little house

in the wood where the old, old Magician lived, and there he was standing at his door.

'Greetings, brave young men!' he cried. 'I see you have been successful in your quest and each have found a wife. And I see also that you have brought the youngest and prettiest for me!'

'She's not for you, you silly old man!' said the young men. 'She is for our youngest brother, as we promised him before we left home.'

'What do I hear?' shrieked the Magician. 'Promised to another? I'll soon make you sorry you ever promised such a thing and cheated me like this!'

So saying he raised his magic wand, muttered a charm, and turned all six brothers and their brides into big grey stones. Only the youngest sister remained unenchanted, and her the Magician took into his house to cook and dust and do all the work for him.

The girl was not altogether unhappy, but she grieved greatly over the loss of her sisters and their husbands, and was dreadfully afraid lest the old, old Magician should die and leave her all alone in the forest with no means of breaking the enchantment.

One day she told him how afraid she was of being left alone if anything should happen to him.

'There is no need to be anxious,' said the Magician. 'You need neither fear my death nor desire it: for I have no heart in my breast. However, if I should happen to die, you have but to take my wand and touch the grey stones, and your sisters and their husbands will be themselves again.'

'If you have no heart,' said the girl, much surprised, 'how is it that you are still alive?'

'It is because I have no heart that I am alive,' smiled the Magician. 'Naturally anyone wanting to kill me would stab me to the heart. But as my heart is not there, they could not do so. No, by my magic I have been able to take out my heart and hide it where it can never be found or harmed.'

'And where is that?' asked the girl.

She had to question him several times, and he returned several false answers before he revealed the truth.

'There is no harm in telling you,' he said at length, 'for you could not possibly find it – nor could anyone else, for I have taken good care of that. Far away from here in a lonely spot stands an ancient church. It has doors of iron, which are never opened, and round it runs a deep moat which is spanned by no bridge. Within that ancient, deserted church a bird flies up and down without ever stopping, for it never eats and never drinks and never dies. No can catch it, and while that bird lives I shall live also: for in it is my heart.'

It was obvious that the Magician's heart was quite safe from his serving girl; and the days passed while she brooded in vain on how she might rescue her sisters and escape from her present position.

And then one day a young traveller came to the door and wished her 'Good day'. The Magician was away from home, as was often the case, and the girl returned the young man's greetings and they fell into talk.

Presently she asked him whence he came and where he was going, and he answered sadly:

'Mine is a sorrowful story. I had six brothers who went away to find brides for themselves, and one for me; but they have never come home, and I am on my way to seek them through the wide world.'

'Oh my dear friend!' cried the girl. 'You need go no further in your quest. Sit down and I will bring you meat and drink, and tell you all you want to know.'

So she told him the whole story of how the six brothers had been bringing her and her six sisters back to their home, when the Magician had caught them and turned them into stones. And she also told him that the Magician had no heart in his body and could only be overcome by someone who could find the lonely church and catch the bird in which his heart was hidden.

'I shall go in search of that bird,' said the young man promptly. 'I feel sure that God will help me to find and catch it so that you may all be freed from this wicked Magician.'

It was getting late by now, so the girl hid the young man for the night; and next morning when the Magician had again gone out into the forest, she sent him on his way with his knapsack filled with provisions.

He walked for some time until it seemed to him that breakfast would be a good idea. So he opened his knapsack and took out some of the good things with which the girl had filled it.

'What a feast!' he exclaimed happily. 'Will anyone come and share it with me?'

'Moo-oo!' said a voice close beside him, and looking up he saw a big red ox, which said: 'I have much pleasure in accepting your kind invitation.'

'I'm delighted to see you,' said the young man. 'Pray, help yourself. All that I have is at your service.'

And so the ox lay down comfortably, and made a hearty meal, and the young man had very little of it.

'Many thanks for your kindness,' said the ox when breakfast was done. 'If you are in danger, or in need of help, call for me and I will do what I can for you.'

Off went the ox among the bushes, and the young man strapped up his knapsack and continued on his way, walking fast and whistling as he went.

Presently the shortening shadows and his own hunger warned him that it was time for lunch, and he sat down in the shade of a tree and took out of his knapsack some more of the good things with which the girl had filled it.

'What a feast!' he cried gaily. 'Will anyone come and share it with me?'

'Umph! Umph!' said a voice close beside him, and out of the thicket ran a wild boar, grunting: 'Did you offer me lunch? Do you really mean me to come and share it?'

'By all means. Help yourself to all I have!' cried the young man gaily; and the two had an excellent lunch together in the shade of the tree: but the young man got very little of it.

'Thank you for your kindness,' said the wild boar when lunch was finished. 'When you are in danger, or in need of help, call for me and I will see what I can do.'

Off went the wild boar among the trees, and the young man continued on his way with a very much lighter knapsack, walking fast and singing happily as he went.

He walked for a long time, and when the shades of evening began to fall he came out of the forest to an open plain with high crags on one side.

He felt hungry again, and having still some provisions left he decided to eat his supper before the light failed.

Pulling out all that was left in his knapsack, he spread it on the ground and exclaimed:

'Well, if not quite a feast, at least there's the makings of a good supper here! Will anyone come and share it with me?'

Scarcely had he spoken when he heard the flapping of heavy wings above him, and a large griffin flew down from the cliffs against the bottom of which he was leaning and said:

'I heard someone offering me a share of a meal: is there really something for me?'

'Certainly there is,' said the young man. 'Come and take all you want, and we ll soon clear away what's left.'

So the griffin ate his fill, and the young man got very little of that supper.

'Call me if you need my help!' said the griffin, swallowing the last mouthful, and away he flew up to the top of the cliff.

'I wish he hadn't been in such a hurry,' thought the young man, 'I would have asked him if he knew the way to the church where the Magician keeps his heart. However, that must keep until morning: it's too dark to go any farther now.'

So the young man groped his way round the bottom of the cliffs until he found a small cave in which he settled down for the night and slept peacefully.

In the morning he came out of the cave rubbing his eyes – and then he rubbed them indeed. For there in front of him was the lonely church completely surrounded by a deep moat without a single bridge by which to cross.

The young man went down to the moat and walked all round it several times. But it was very deep, and it was no use trying to swim it as the walls of the church went straight down into the water, and the only door which was on a level with the water, had not so much as a doorstep on which he could stand.

'I think the ox might be able to help me, if only he was here!' exclaimed the young man.

Scarcely had he spoken when the ox came galloping out of the forest, across the plain to where he stood, and began drinking up the water. And very soon the moat was completely dry.

The young man went down into it, and found that the walls of the church continued right to the bottom. But he could not climb up them; and the door high above his head was sheathed and barred with iron.

'I think the wild boar might be able to help me, if only he were here,' exclaimed the young man.

Scarcely had he spoken when he heard the sound of footsteps rushing across the plain, and a moment later the wild boar leapt down into the dry moat and began digging a hole through the foundations of the church with his big sharp tusks. And very soon he had made a passage by which the young man was able to walk quite easily up into the church.

As soon as he stood in the nave, the young man saw a single bird flying backwards and forwards, backwards and forwards, high above him, without ever stopping.

'I think the griffin would be able to catch it, if only he were here!' exclaimed the young man.

There came a rasping of feathers in the passage which the wild boar had dug, and a moment later the griffin was in the church. And it did not take him long to catch the bird and give it to the young man, who promptly popped it into his empty knapsack and fastened the straps firmly.

Then, having thanked his three friends for their help, he went back through the passage, up the farther bank of the dry moat, away across the plain and through the forest until he came to the Magician's house.

It was not quite evening, so the Magician had not yet returned home, and the young man had time for a bite and a sup during which he told the girl all that had happened.

But they had no time to make any plans before she exclaimed suddenly: 'I hear the Magician coming! Quick, hide under the bed with the bird in your bag, and keep as quiet as you can!'

The young man had just time enough to do so, when the Magician came in, sighing and groaning:

'I feel so ill!' he said, 'the bird which holds my heart must have been caught by somebody and put in a cage. My heart is no longer free: my heart is aching, and nothing will go well with me any more.'

Hearing this, the young man gave his knapsack a squeeze, thinking to frighten the Magician into lifting the spell and letting them all go home in safety.

But he squeezed rather harder than he meant, and the Magician gave a loud cry and exclaimed:

'Oh death is gripping me! My heart is breaking! Oh what a dreadful pain in my heart!'

So saying he staggered back and fell on the bed – which at once gave way. With great difficulty the young man dragged himself out from underneath, and pulled the knapsack out after him – only to find that when the Magician fell on the bed and the bed fell on him, he had fallen on it, and the bird was squashed flat and quite dead.

He turned to look at the Magician and found that he was dead too: for he could not live longer than his heart which had died with the bird.

Quickly the young man snatched up the Magician's wand and ran out into the garden. There he struck the grey stones with it, one by one, and at once they turned back into his six brothers and their six beautiful wives.

So they all returned home happily; and the seventh brother married the seventh sister, and they were the happiest of them all.

The Wizard King

This is one of the Fairy stories made up and told at the French Court in the years before the French Revolution. The stories were often based on the traditional Fairy Tales handed down by French peasants, but would really be classed as invented, literary tales. They were collected in Le Cabinet des Fées in forty-one volumes, published between 1785 and 1789. The most famous of these was 'Beauty and the Beast', as long as a novel in the original, but speedily retold in the simple fairy-tale form which we all know so well. With such an example before us, little excuse is needed for treating the present tale in the same way.

In very ancient times there lived a King who was powerful not only on account of his great wealth, his wide domains and the strength of his army, but also on account of his magic: for besides being a King, he was also a Wizard.

This being so, there was no monarch who dared refuse him as a suitor for his daughter's hand in marriage, and the Wizard King was able to choose the fairest Princess living – the more so because, by his magic, he was able to assume any shape he chose and so, in the form of some bird such as an eagle, to visit all parts of the world without difficulty.

The Princess whom he married was not unhappy at his Court, and when a little Prince was born to her, she had no further regrets at being married to a Wizard. But she had a few anxieties; and for the sake of her child she made haste at the first opportunity to visit her Fairy Godmother in secret.

She was forced to do this without the King knowing because all Good Fairies were the enemies of anyone who practised Black Magic – and all Wizards hated the Fairies and would do anything in their power to work them evil.

The Fairy gave the Prince the gift of pleasing everybody

THE WIZARD KING 149

whom he met and of learning easily anything to which he set his mind. But she warned him not to have anything to do with Black Magic, and promised to help him if he ever needed a charm to protect him from his father the Wizard King.

The Prince passed a happy childhood and became the delight of all his teachers and tutors. But a great sorrow befell him when he was still a boy, in the death of his mother. The Wizard King was even more heartbroken by the loss of his Queen, and he spent less and less of his time at home, and more and more of it flying about the world in the form of a great eagle.

Often, when he reached a distant land, he would remain there for many weeks in some other shape, seeing strange things and learning new arts before returning to his own kingdom to make sure that all was well there and that no rebellion was being prepared.

One day as the Wizard King was on his travels in the form of an eagle he came to a country which he had never before visited, where it seemed always to be spring, and the air full of scent of jessamine and orange blossoms. Attracted by the sweet perfume he flew lower, and perceived some large and beautiful gardens filled with rarest flowers, and with fountains throwing up their clear waters into the air in a hundred different shapes. A wide stream flowed through the garden, and on it floated richly decorated barges and gondolas filled with people dressed in splendid clothes sewn with jewels and golden threads.

In one of these barges sat the Queen of that country with her only daughter, a maiden as beautiful as the day, attended by the ladies of the Court. Even in the form of an eagle, with eyes that could look upon the sun without blinking, the Wizard King was dazzled by the beauty of this Princess. He perched on the top of a large orange tree and gazed and gazed at her until there seemed to him to be nothing in the world more desirable than to make this beautiful Princess his next Queen.

An eagle who is really a King does not lack for boldness, and if that King is also a Wizard he does not think of right or wrong, but only of his own desires. Very soon the Wizard King came to the conclusion that he must have the Princess, and that the best and easiest way to do so was to carry her off.

So he waited until he saw her in the act of stepping from the barge, and swooped down and snatched her up in his strong talons before the attendant on the side could reach out his hand to help her from the boat.

On finding herself being carried away into the sky by this mighty bird, the Princess cried out most piteously. But the Wizard King needed all his strength to carry her, and had no breath to utter a word of comfort, though he was sorry for her fright.

At length, when they were far away from her native land, the Wizard King alighted in a flowery meadow and set the Princess gently on the ground.

When he had recovered his breath he said to her: 'Beautiful Princess, do not be afraid. I am no ordinary bird, but the King of a great country who has chosen you to be my Queen and am carrying you to your new kingdom.'

The Princess was speechless with amazement for a few moments. But then she burst into tears and would not be comforted.

'Do not cry,' begged the Wizard King. 'My only wish is to make you the happiest person in the world.'

'If you speak the truth, my lord,' sobbed the Princess, 'please take me home at once and restore me to liberty and to my beloved parents. Otherwise I can only look upon you as my worst enemy.'

'Your words would fill me with despair, if I believed them,' answered the Wizard King. 'But I am taking you to a life of

pleasure and delight, where you shall have whatever you wish, and will be served with honour and respect by your new subjects.'

So saying, and regardless of her cries, he carried her up into the sky again, and at length brought her to earth not far from the capital city of his kingdom.

The Princess found herself in a lonely valley among the mountains. But the Wizard King did not intend to leave her in solitude. He plucked a feather from his breast, and at once resumed his own form: a tall, handsome man, though quite old enough to be her father, and with the hard look in his eyes of someone who has always had his own way, and never considered the feelings of anyone else in the getting of it.

But the Princess still felt nothing but hatred for her captor, and hated him scarcely less when by his magic he conjured up a beautiful palace to which he led her and presented her to dozens of slave girls who were ready to do her slightest wish.

Although pleased that she was not to be left in the lonely valley, or even in an uninhabited palace, the Princess drew small comfort from all the treasures that were heaped upon her by the Wizard King, and still less from the pretty attendants, however ready they were to obey her slightest command. Indeed, her greatest comfort during her long days and nights in the enchanted palace was a brilliantly coloured parrot with a remarkable gift of speech which she found there.

For the Wizard King kept her a prisoner in the palace, surrounding it with a dense cloud so that no one could find it, and visiting her whenever he could leave his own Court, to beg her again and again to become his wife.

But she refused him steadfastly; and before long the Wizard King began to suspect that she was in love with someone else. For he could not believe that any other reason would prevent a young Princess from accepting anyone as important, wealthy and magically endowed as himself.

Soon he came to the conclusion that the Prince his son must somehow have penetrated the magic cloud which surrounded the palace and charmed the Princess with the goodness, youth and beauty which made all the Court adore him.

Filled with jealousy that soon began turning into hate, the Wizard King made haste to send his son away on a visit to the Courts of several neighbouring Kings in search of a Princess to be his bride.

The Prince passed swiftly from Court to Court without falling in love with any of the lovely Princesses to whom he was introduced. But in time he came to the Court of the King and Queen whose daughter had been carried off by the eagle, where she was still bitterly lamented, being her parents' only child and deeply loved by all their subjects.

This King and Queen, though still in deep mourning, entertained the Prince very graciously, being charmed by his kindness and genuine goodness. And one day they took him to their private room where, the moment he entered, he was struck dumb by the portrait of the most beautiful Princess he had ever seen.

'That is the picture of our beloved daughter, who is lost to us,' said the Queen, and burst into tears, while the King told the Prince the whole tragic story of the gigantic eagle who had carried her off, they knew neither where nor how.

The Prince gazed for a long time on the picture. Then he said quietly:

'I shall not rest, nor turn aside for anything else until I have found the Princess your daughter. And if I never find her I will continue in quest of her all my life. For her only do I love and she only shall be my bride – or no one.'

'Only find our daughter,' said the King, 'and she shall be yours. And after my death this kingdom shall be yours and hers – for we have no other children.'

So the Prince set out in quest of the lost Princess. And the very first thing he did was to seek his mother's Fairy Godmother, tell her all the story and implore her help and advice.

'I cannot fly to rescue the Princess,' said the Fairy, 'because she is held by the evil enchantment of a Wizard. But you can pass safely and undiscovered through the cloud of darkness which surrounds the enchanted palace in which she is kept prisoner, and prepare her for her escape. But you must go in disguise ... Let me see ... Yes, I have it! Wait just a few days, and we will have the perfect disguise for you.'

The Fairy knew more than she told the Prince, for she did not wish him to realize just yet that it was his own father, the Wizard King, who had stolen the Princess. She also knew that the Princess's parrot flew occasionally out through the cloud into the wide world outside. And before long she was able to capture it and bring it to her own palace.

Here by a simple charm in White Magic she was able to change the Prince into a parrot exactly like the Princess's Pet – and away he flew.

Through the cloud of darkness he went, found the enchanted palace and soon discovered the room where the Princess sat sadly mourning her lost freedom and wondering where her one companion had gone.

To begin with the Prince said only such things to the Princess as a parrot might say. And indeed he was so overwhelmed by her beauty that he was almost tongue-tied.

It was a good thing that he had not made himself known at once, for suddenly the Wizard King arrived and again began begging the Princess to become his wife. Still she refused, and at length the Wizard King flew into a towering rage: 'This is your last chance!' he cried. 'I'll give you until this time tomorrow to change your mind – and if you do not marry me willingly I'll see what force can do – force and the use of some of the more unpleasant charms of which I am the master!'

So saying, he changed himself into a hawk and sped out of the window and home to the dark tower above his own palace where all that night he was busy preparing potions and philtres for the morrow.

When he had gone the parrot flew on to the stool in front of the Princess and said:

'Beautiful Princess, there is no time to tell you all my story. Suffice it to say that I come from your father and mother to save you from the Wizard King. I am myself a Prince, disguised like this by a Good Fairy, and she has given me a charm with which to rescue you. Pluck the little white feather from among the green ones on my right wing and set it to your lips . . .'

The Princess was rather startled at the parrot's words, and at first she would not believe him, fearing lest this should be some cruel trick devised by the Wizard King. But the disguised Prince told her so many things that only her parents knew that at last she realized that he had indeed come from them.

So she plucked out the white feather and set it to her lips. At once she too was changed into a parrot; and the two birds flew easily out of the window, across the palace garden and through the cloud of darkness which surrounded it.

Once beyond the cloud of evil magic they found the Fairy waiting for them in her flying chariot drawn by a team of eagles. As soon as they were seated in it she waved her wand and Prince and Princess were restored to their natural shapes.

Then she flew off with them over the wide world to the palace of the Princess's parents. And short though the journey was, it was long enough for the Prince and Princess to fall deeply in love with one another, and confess that neither could ever marry anyone else.

The moment they reached the Palace of the King and Queen the Fairy sprang from her chariot exclaiming:

'This brave Prince has rescued your daughter from the Wizard King who stole her away in the shape of an eagle. There is no time now to thank him, or to rejoice over her safe return. My advice to you is that these two young people should be married immediately: for the Wizard King will be here before long, and we must be prepared for him.'

The King and Queen saw the urgency of this and acted promptly. And scarcely were the Prince and Princess married when the Wizard King arrived like a thundercloud in his usual disguise of a gigantic eagle.

When he saw that the Princess was married, and who the bridegroom was, his rage was so great that he let the disguise slip from him and stood before them in his own form.

'You have robbed me of my bride to be!' he cried. 'You

are no longer a son of mine! And thus I punish you and punish this ungrateful girl who has thrown away a kingdom and the love of such a Wizard as I am for the sake of a wretched boy!'

So saying he took a pinch of black dust from his pouch and cast it towards the Prince and Princess, muttering an incantation as he did.

But the Fairy was watching. Before the dust could touch either the Prince or Princess she waved her wand and a sudden breeze sprang up between them and blew it back into the face of the Wizard King.

In a moment he shrivelled up and turned into a black vampire bat which flew squeaking from the window and away towards the distant mountains to find a cave where it could hide from the light of day. And that was the last that was ever seen of the Wizard King.

'Had the dust touched you,' said the Fairy solemnly, 'you would both have shrivelled away into nothing. His magic was too strong for that to happen to him. But this is better. He no longer has any power, nor will he return: but he has still time to repent of his evil deeds.'

So the Prince did not mourn overmuch for the loss of his father. Instead, he led his bride back to the kingdom which was now his – and they lived out their days in great happiness, adding the Princess's kingdom to the Prince's in the fulness of time. And in either kingdom the most welcome guest at any time was the Good Fairy who had saved them from the magic of the Wizard King.

Chinook and Chinok

ANDREW LANG

Chinook and Chinok were magicians of merit
Who each of them kept a familiar spirit;
They lived, we should tell you, a long while ago,
Between the Red Men and the wild Eskimo;
And the feats of the common magicians they'd mock,
Of the noisy *Pow-wow** and the dark *Angekok*,†
But the best of good friends were Chinook and Chinok!

It was nothing to either to fly in the air,
To float like a fish, or to climb like a bear.
It was nothing to either to change by a wish,
His foes into fowls, and his friends into fish!
Thought Chinook, 'I shall ask old Chinok to a feast,
And charm him, for fun, to the shape of a beast,
And when I have laughed at his fright till I'm black,
Why – dear old Chinok! I will alter him back.'
So he sent to Chinok, and he asked him to dine.
Thought Chinok to himself, 'I've an artful design,
For I'll change old Chinook into some sort of beast,
And I'll soon change him back at the end of the feast!'

So they met, and their medicine-bags laid on the shelf,
But each had a powder he kept to himself,
A powder for making his friend look absurd
By changing him into a beast or a bird,
While each in his medicine-bag stored up another,
By which he'd restore his old shape to his brother.

* A *Pow-wow* is a Red Indian magician.
† An *Angekok* is an Eskimo magician.

Then both, when they settled serenely to eat,
Dropped a pinch of the powder unseen on the meat;
And Chinook, with a grin, began making his mock:
'Why, you're changing,' he cried, 'to a badger, Chinok.'
And Chinok, who felt rather uneasy, cried 'Look!
You are changing yourself to a toad, my Chinook!'

Then each of them longed to return to himself,
But the bags with the powders were high on the shelf,
And the badger can't climb, and the toad could not hop,
To the shelf where the medicine-bags lay on the top,
So the pair could not reach them by hook or by crook,
And a badger and toad are Chinok and Chinook!

Yes, a toad and a badger those worthies remain,
And the moral of all is uncommonly plain,
That good luck never comes to a person who pokes
At a host, or a guest, his dull practical jokes!

PART FOUR
Magicians of Later Days

The Castle of Kerglas

EMILE SOUVESTRE
(translated by Mrs Andrew Lang)

PERONNIK was a poor idiot who belonged to nobody, and he would have died of starvation if it had not been for the kindness of the village people, who gave him food whenever he chose to ask for it. And as for a bed, when night came, and he grew sleepy, he looked about for a heap of straw, and making a hole in it, crept in, like a lizard. Idiot though he was, he was never unhappy, but always thanked gratefully those who fed him, and sometimes would stop for a little and sing to them. For he could imitate a lark so well, that no one knew which was Peronnik and which was the bird.

He had been wandering in a forest one day for several hours, and when evening approached, he suddenly felt very hungry. Luckily, just at that place the trees grew thinner, and he could see a small farmhouse a little way off. Peronnik went straight towards it, and found the farmer's wife standing at the door holding in her hands the large bowl out of which her children had eaten their supper.

'I am hungry, will you give me something to eat?' asked the boy.

'If you can find anything here, you are welcome to it,' answered she, and, indeed, there was not much left, as everybody's spoon had dipped in. But Peronnik ate what was there with a hearty appetite, and thought that he had never tasted better food.

'It is made of the finest flour and mixed with the richest milk and stirred by the best cook in all the countryside,' and though he said it to himself, the woman heard him.

'Poor innocent,' she murmured, 'he does not know what

he is saying, but I will cut him a slice of that new wheaten loaf,' and so she did, and Peronnik ate up every crumb, and declared that nobody less than the bishop's baker could have baked it. This flattered the farmer's wife so much that she gave him some butter to spread on it, and Peronnik was still eating it on the doorstep when an armed knight rode up.

'Can you tell me the way to the castle of Kerglas?' asked he.

'To Kerglas? Are you *really* going to Kerglas?' cried the woman, turning pale.

'Yes; and in order to get there I have come from a country so far off that it has taken me three months' hard riding to travel as far as this.'

'And why do you want to go to Kerglas?' said she.

'I am seeking the basin of gold and the lance of diamonds which are in the castle,' he answered.

Then Peronnik looked up. 'The basin and the lance are very costly things,' he said suddenly.

'More costly and precious than all the crowns in the world,' replied the stranger, 'for not only will the basin furnish you with the best food that you can dream of, but if you drink of

it, it will cure you of any illness however dangerous, and will even bring the dead back to life, if it touches their mouths. As to the diamond lance, that will cut through any stone or metal.'

'And to whom do these wonders belong?' asked Peronnik in amazement.

'To a magician named Rogear who lives in the castle,' answered the woman. 'Every day he passes along here, mounted on a black mare, with a colt thirteen months old trotting behind. But no one dares to attack him, as he always carries his lance.'

'That is true,' said the knight, 'but there is a spell laid upon him which forbids his using it within the castle of Kerglas. The moment he enters, the basin and lance are put away in a dark cellar which no key but one can open. And *that* is the place where i wish to fight the magician.'

'You will never overcome him, Sir Knight,' replied the woman, shaking her head. 'More than a hundred gentlemen have ridden past this house bent on the same errand, and not one has ever come back.'

'I know that, good woman,' returned the knight, 'but then they did not have, like me, instructions from the hermit of Blavet.'

'And what did the hermit tell you?' asked Peronnik.

'He told me that I should have to pass through a wood full of all sorts of enchantments and voices, which would try to frighten me and make me lose my way. Most of those who have gone before me have wandered they know not where, and perished from cold, hunger, or fatigue.'

'Well, suppose you get through safely?' said the idiot.

'If I do,' continued the knight, 'I shall then meet a sort of fairy armed with a needle of fire which burns to ashes all it touches. This dwarf stands guarding an apple-tree, from which I am bound to pluck an apple.'

'And next?' inquired Peronnik.

'Next I shall find the flower that laughs, protected by a lion whose mane is formed of vipers. I must pluck that flower, and go on to the lake of the dragons and fight the black man who holds in his hand the iron ball which never misses its mark and returns of its own accord to its master. After that, I enter the valley of pleasure, where some who conquered all the other obstacles have left their bones. If I can win through this, I shall reach a river with only one ford, where a lady in black will be seated. She will mount my horse behind me, and tell me what I am to do next.'

He paused, and the woman shook her head.

'You will never be able to do all that,' said she, but he bade her remember that these were only matters for men, and galloped away down the path she pointed out.

The farmer's wife sighed and, giving Peronnik some more food, bade him good-night. The idiot rose and was opening the gate which led into the forest when the farmer himself came up.

'I want a boy to tend my cattle,' he said abruptly, 'as the one I had has run away. Will you stay and do it?' and Peronnik, though he loved his liberty and hated work, recollected the good food he had eaten, and agreed to stop.

At sunrise he collected his herd carefully and led them to the rich pasture which lay along the borders of the forest, cutting himself a hazel wand with which to keep them in order.

His task was not quite so easy as it looked, for the cows had a way of straying into the wood, and by the time he had brought one back another was off. He had gone some distance into the trees, after a naughty black cow which gave him more trouble than all the rest, when he heard the noise of horses' feet, and peeping through the leaves he beheld the giant Rogear seated on his mare, with the colt trotting behind. Round the giant's neck hung the golden bowl suspended from a chain, and in his hand he grasped the diamond lance, which gleamed like fire. But as soon as he was out of sight the idiot sought in vain for traces of the path he had taken.

This happened not only once but many times, till Peronnik grew so used to him that he never troubled to hide. But on each occasion he saw him the desire to possess the bowl and the lance became stronger.

One evening the boy was sitting alone on the edge of the forest, when a man with a white beard stopped beside him.

'Do you want to know the way to Kerglas?' asked the idiot, and the man answered, 'I know it well.'

'You have been there without being killed by the magician?' cried Peronnik.

'Oh! he had nothing to fear from me,' replied the white-bearded man, 'I am Rogear's elder brother, the wizard Bryak. When I wish to visit him I always pass this way, and as even I cannot go through the enchanted wood without losing myself, I call the colt to guide me.' Stooping down as he spoke he traced three circles on the ground and murmured some words very low, which Peronnik could not hear. Then he added aloud:

> Colt, free to run and free to eat,
> Colt, gallop fast until we meet,

and instantly, the colt appeared, frisking and jumping to the wizard, who threw a halter over his neck and leapt on his back.

Peronnik kept silence at the farm about this adventure, but he understood very well that if he was ever to get to Kerglas he must first catch the colt which knew the way. Unhappily he had not heard the magic words uttered by the wizard, and he could not manage to draw the three circles, so if he was to summon the colt at all he must invent some other means of doing it.

All day long, while he was herding the cows, he thought

and thought how he was to call the colt, for he felt sure that once on its back he could overcome the other dangers. Meantime he must be ready in case a chance should come, and he made his preparations at night, when everyone was asleep. Remembering what he had seen the wizard do, he patched up an old halter that was hanging in a corner of the stable, twisted a rope of hemp to catch the colt's feet, and a net such as is used for snaring birds. Next he sewed roughly together some bits of cloth to serve as a pocket, and this he filled with glue and lark's feathers, a string of beads, a whistle of elder wood, and a slice of bread rubbed over with bacon fat. Then he went out to the path down which Rogear, his mare, and the colt always rode, and crumbled the bread on one side of it.

Punctual to their hour all three appeared, eagerly watched by Peronnik, who lay hid in the bushes close by. Suppose it was useless; suppose the mare, and not the colt, ate the crumbs? Suppose – but no! the mare and her rider went safely by, vanishing round a corner, while the colt, trotting along with its head on the ground, smelt the bread, and began greedily to lick up the pieces. Oh, how good it was! Why had no one ever given it that before, and so absorbed was the little beast, sniffing about after a few more crumbs, that it never heard Peronnik creep up till it felt the halter on its neck and the rope round its feet, and – in another moment – someone on its back.

Going as fast as the hobbles would allow, the colt turned into one of the wildest parts of the forest, while its rider sat trembling at the strange sights he saw. Sometimes the earth seemed to open in front of them and he was looking into a bottomless pit; sometimes the trees burst into flames and he found himself in the midst of a fire; often in the act of crossing a stream the water rose and threatened to sweep him away; and again, at the foot of a mountain, great rocks would roll towards him, as if they would crush him and his colt beneath their weight. To his dying day Peronnik never knew whether these things were real or if he only imagined them, but he pulled down his knitted cap so as to cover his eyes, and trusted the colt to carry him down the right road.

At last the forest was left behind, and they came out on a wide plain where the air blew fresh and strong. The idiot ventured to peep out, and found to his relief that the enchantments seemed to have ended, though a thrill of horror shot through him as he noticed the skeletons of men scattered over the plain, beside the skeletons of their horses. And what were those grey forms trotting away in the distance? Were they – could they be – *wolves*?

But vast though the plain seemed, it did not take long to cross, and very soon the colt entered a sort of shady park in which was standing a single apple-tree, its branches bowed down to the ground with the weight of its fruit. In front was the korigan – the little fairy man – holding in his hand the fiery sword, which reduced to ashes everything it touched. At the sight of Peronnik he uttered a piercing scream, and raised his sword, but without appearing surprised the youth only lifted his cap, though he took care to remain at a little distance.

'Do not be alarmed, my prince,' said Peronnik, 'I am just on my way to Kerglas, as the noble Rogear has begged me to come to him on business.'

'Begged *you* to come!' repeated the dwarf, 'and who, then, are you?'

'I am the new servant he has engaged, as you know very well,' answered Peronnik.

'I do not know at all,' rejoined the korigan sulkily, 'and you may be a robber for all I can tell.'

'I am so sorry,' replied Peronnik, 'but I may be wrong in calling myself a servant, for I am only a bird-catcher. But do not delay me, I pray, for his highness the magician expects me, and, as you see, has lent me his colt so that I may reach the castle all the quicker.'

At these words the korigan cast his eyes for the first time on the colt, which he knew to be the one belonging to the magician, and began to think that the young man was speaking the truth. After examining the horse, he studied the rider, who had such an innocent, and indeed vacant, air that he appeared incapable of inventing a story. Still, the dwarf did

not feel *quite* sure that all was right, and asked what the magician wanted with a bird-catcher.

'From what he says, he wants one very badly,' replied Peronnik, 'as he declares that all his grain and all the fruit in his garden at Kerglas are eaten up by the birds.'

'And how are you going to stop that, my fine fellow?' inquired the korigan; and Peronnik showed him the snare he had prepared, and remarked that no bird could possibly escape from it.

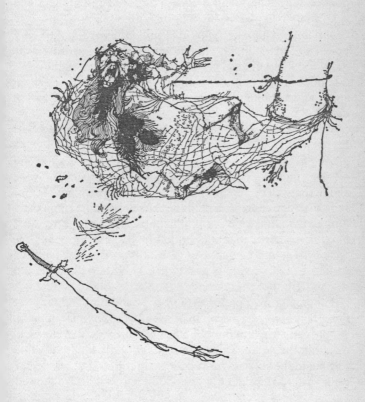

'That is just what I should like to be sure of,' answered the korigan. 'My apples are completely eaten up by blackbirds and thrushes. Lay your snare, and if you can manage to catch them, I will let you pass.'

'That is a fair bargain,' and as he spoke Peronnik jumped down and fastened his colt to a tree; then, stooping, he fixed one end of the net to the trunk of the apple tree, and called to the korigan to hold the other while he took out the pegs. The dwarf did as he was bid, when suddenly Peronnik threw the noose over his neck and drew it close, and the korigan was held as fast as any of the birds he wished to snare.

Shrieking with rage, he tried to undo the cord, but he only pulled the knot tighter. He had put down the sword on the grass, and Peronnik had been careful to fix the net on the other side of the tree, so that it was now easy for him to pluck an apple, and to mount his horse, without being hindered by the dwarf, whom he left to his fate.

When they had left the plain behind them, Peronnik and his steed found themselves in a narrow valley in which was a grove of trees, full of all sorts of sweet-smelling things – roses of every colour, yellow broom, pink honeysuckle – while above them all towered a wonderful scarlet pansy whose face bore a strange expression. This was the flower that laughs, and no one who looked at it could help laughing too. Peronnik's heart beat high at the thought that he had reached safely the second trial, and he gazed quite calmly at the lion with the mane of vipers twisting and twirling, who walked up and down in front of the grove.

The young man pulled up and removed his cap, for, idiot though he was, he knew that when you have to do with people greater than yourself, a cap is more useful in the hand than on the head. Then, after wishing all kinds of good fortune to the lion and his family, he inquired if he was on the right road to Kerglas.

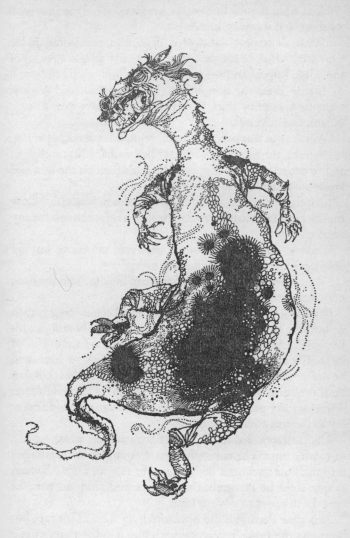

'And what is your business at Kerglas?' asked the lion with a growl, and showing his teeth.

'With all respect,' answered Peronnik, pretending to be very frightened, 'I am the servant of a lady who is a friend of the noble Rogear and sends him some larks for a pasty.'

'Larks?' cried the lion, licking his long whiskers. 'Why, it must be a century since I have had any! Have you a large quantity with you?'

'As many as this bag will hold,' replied Peronnik, opening, as he spoke, the bag which he had filled with feathers and glue; and to prove what he said, he turned his back on the lion and began to imitate the song of a lark.

'Come,' exclaimed the lion, whose mouth watered, 'show me the birds! I should like to see if they are fat enough for my master.'

'I would do it with pleasure,' answered the idiot, 'but if I once open the bag they will all fly away.'

'Well, open it wide enough for me to look in,' said the lion, drawing a little nearer.

Now this was just what Peronnik had been hoping for, so he held the bag while the lion opened it carefully and put his head right inside, so that he might get a good mouthful of larks. But the mass of feathers and glue stuck to him, and before he could pull his head out again Peronnik had drawn tight the cord, and tied it in a knot that no man could untie. Then, quickly gathering the flower that laughs, he rode off as fast as the colt could take him.

The path soon led to the lake of the dragons, which he had to swim across. The colt, who was accustomed to it, plunged into the water without hesitation; but as soon as the dragons caught sight of Peronnik they approached from all parts of the lake in order to devour him.

This time Peronnik did not trouble to take off his cap, but he threw the beads he carried with him into the water as you throw black corn to a duck, and with each bead that he swallowed a dragon turned on his back and died, so that the idiot reached the other side without further trouble.

The valley guarded by the black man now lay before him, and from afar Peronnik beheld him, chained by one foot to a rock at the entrance, and holding the iron ball which never missed its mark and always returned to its master's hand. In his head the black man had six eyes that were never all shut at once, but kept watch one after the other. At this moment they were all open and Peronnik knew well that if the black man caught a glimpse of him he would cast his ball. So, hiding the colt behind a thicket of bushes, he crawled along a ditch and crouched close to the very rock to which the black man was chained.

The day was hot, and after a while the man began to grow sleepy. Two of his eyes closed, and Peronnik sang gently. In a moment a third eye shut, and Peronnik sang on. The lid of a fourth eye dropped heavily, and then those of the fifth and the sixth. The black man was asleep altogether.

Then, on tiptoe, the idiot crept back to the colt, which he led over soft moss past the black man into the vale of pleasure, a delicious garden full of fruits that dangled before your mouth, fountains running with wine, and flowers chanting in soft little voices. Further on, tables were spread with food, and girls dancing on the grass called to him to join them.

Peronnik heard, and, scarcely knowing what he did, drew the colt into a slower pace. He sniffed greedily the smell of the dishes, and raised his head the better to see the dancers. Another instant and he would have stopped altogether and been lost, like others before him, when suddenly there came to him like a vision the golden bowl and the diamond lance. Drawing his whistle from his pocket, he blew it loudly, so as to drown the sweet sounds about him, and ate what was left of his bread and bacon to still the craving of the magic fruits.

His eyes he fixed steadily on the ears of the colt, that he might not see the dancers.

In this way he was able to reach the end of the garden, and at length perceived the castle of Kerglas, with the river between them which had only one ford. Would the lady be there, as the old man had told him? Yes, surely that was she, sitting on a rock, in a black satin dress, and her face the colour of a Moorish woman's. The idiot rode up, and took off his cap more politely than ever, and asked if she did not wish to cross the river.

'I was waiting for you to help me do so,' answered she. 'Come near, that I may get up behind you.'

Peronnik did as she bade him, and by the help of his arm she jumped nimbly on to the back of the colt.

'Do you know how to kill the magician?' asked the lady, as they were crossing the ford.

'I thought that, being a magician, he was immortal, and that no one could kill him,' replied Peronnik.

'Persuade him to taste that apple, and he will die, and if that is not enough I will touch him with my finger, for I am the plague,' answered she.

'But if I kill him, how am I to get the golden bowl and the diamond lance that are hidden in the cellar without a key?' rejoined Peronnik.

'The flower that laughs opens all doors and lightens all darkness,' said the lady; and as she spoke, they reached the further bank, and advanced towards the castle.

In front of the entrance was a sort of tent supported on poles, and under it the giant was sitting, basking in the sun. As soon as he noticed the colt bearing Peronnik and the lady, he lifted his head, and cried in a voice of thunder:

'Why, it is surely the idiot, riding my colt thirteen months old!'

'Greatest of magicians, you are right,' answered Peronnik.

'And how did you manage to catch him?' asked the giant.

'By repeating what I learnt from your brother Bryak on the edge of the forest,' replied the idiot. 'I just said:

> Colt, free to run and free to eat,
> Colt, gallop fast until we meet,

and it came directly.'

'You know my brother, then?' inquired the giant. 'Tell me why he sent you here.'

'To bring you two gifts which he has just received from the country of the Moors,' answered Peronnik: 'the apple of delight and the woman of submission. If you eat the apple you will not desire anything else, and if you take the woman as your servant you will never wish for another.'

'Well, give me the apple, and bid the woman get down,' answered Rogear.

The idiot obeyed, but at the first taste of the apple the giant staggered, and as the long yellow finger of the woman touched him he fell dead.

Leaving the magician where he lay, Peronnik entered the palace, bearing with him the flower that laughs. Fifty doors flew open before him, and at length he reached a long flight of steps which seemed to lead into the bowels of the earth. Down these he went till he came to a silver door without a bar or key. Then he held up high the flower that laughs, and the door slowly swung back, displaying a deep cavern, which was as bright as day from the shining of the golden bowl and the diamond lance. The idiot hastily ran forward and hung the bowl round his neck from the chain which was attached to it, and took the lance in his hand. As he did so, the ground shook beneath him, and with an awful rumbling the palace disappeared, and Peronnik found himself standing close to the forest where he led the cattle to graze.

Though darkness was coming on, Peronnik never thought

of entering the farm, but followed the road which led to the court of the duke of Brittany. As he passed through the town of Vannes he stopped at a tailor's shop, and bought a beautiful costume of brown velvet and a white horse, which he paid for with a handful of gold that he had picked up in the corridor of the castle of Kerglas. Thus he made his way to the city of Nantes, which at that moment was besieged by the French.

A little way off, Peronnik stopped and looked about him. For miles round the country was bare, for the enemy had cut down every tree and burnt every blade of corn; and, idiot though he might be, Peronnik was able to grasp that inside the gates men were dying of famine. He was still gazing with horror, when a trumpeter appeared on the walls, and, after blowing a loud blast, announced that the duke would adopt as his heir the man who could drive the French out of the country.

On the four sides of the city the trumpeter blew his blast, and the last time Peronnik, who had ridden up as close as he might, answered him.

'You need blow no more,' said he, 'for I myself will free the town from her enemies.' And turning to a soldier who came running up, waving his sword, he touched him with the magic lance, and he fell dead on the spot. The men who were following stood still, amazed. Their comrade's armour had not been pierced, of that they were sure, yet he was dead, as if he had been struck to the heart. But before they had time to recover from their astonishment, Peronnik cried out:

'You see how my foes will fare; now behold what I can do for my friends,' and, stooping down, he laid the golden bowl against the mouth of the soldier, who sat up as well as ever. Then, jumping his horse across the trench, he entered the gate of the city, which had opened wide enough to receive him.

The news of these marvels quickly spread through the town, and put fresh spirit into the garrison, so that they declared themselves able to fight under the command of the young stranger. And as the bowl restored all the dead Bretons to life, Peronnik soon had an army large enough to drive away the French, and fulfilled his promise of delivering his country.

As to the bowl and the lance, no one knows what became of them. But some say that Bryak the sorcerer managed to steal them again, and that anyone who wishes to possess them must seek them as Peronnik did.

The Magician and his Pupil

From the German of AMELIA GODIN

THERE was once a poor shoemaker renowned far and wide as a drunkard. He had a good wife and many daughters, but only one son. As soon as this son was old enough his mother dressed him in his best clothes, combed his hair until it shone, and then led him far, far away; for she wished to take him to the capital, and there apprentice him to a master who would teach him a really good trade.

When they had accomplished about half their journey they met a man in black, who asked whither they were going and the object of their journey. On being told, he offered to take the boy as his apprentice, but as he had not given the customary Christian greeting, and would not mention the name of his trade, also because the mother thought there was a wicked gleam in his eyes, she declined to trust him with her son. As he persisted in his offer they were rude, then he troubled them no further.

Shortly after leaving the old man, the boy and his mother came to a wide stretch of land, solitary and barren as a desert, over which they journeyed until hunger, thirst, and fatigue compelled them to rest. Exhausted, they sank on the sandy ground and wept bitterly. Suddenly, at a short distance from them arose a large stone, on whose surface stood a dish of smoking roast beef, a loaf of white bread, and a jug of foaming ale.

Eagerly the weary travellers hastened forward. Alas! the moment they moved, meat and drink vanished, leaving the stone bare and barren; but as soon as they stepped back, the food again made its appearance. After this had happened several times the shoemaker's son guessed what was at the bottom of it. Pointing his stick of aspen wood – a wood, by the way, very powerful against enchantment – he cautiously approached the stone, and thrust his stick into that place on the earth where the shadow of the stone rested.

Immediately the stone with everything on it disappeared, and in the place where the shadow had lain stood the stranger in black who had met them earlier in the day. He bowed politely to the youth and requested him to remove his stick.

'No, that I will not do! This time the stone has met its match! You are a magician, or at least a necromancer. You locked us in this desert and amused yourself with our misery. Now you shall be treated as you deserve. You shall stand here for a year and six weeks, until you are as dry as the stick with which I have nailed you to the earth.'

'Loose me, I entreat you.'

'Yes, on certain conditions! First, you must once more become a stone, and on the stone must appear everything we have already seen.'

The magician immediately vanished, and in his stead appeared the stone covered with a white cloth, and bearing the hot roast beef, white bread, and foaming ale, of which the travellers ate and drank to their hearts' content. When they had finished the stone became the man in black, who entreated piteously to be unnailed.

'I will unnail you directly,' said the youth, 'but only on one condition. You must take me as apprentice for three years, as you yourself formerly proposed, and give me a pledge that you will really teach me all your art.'

The magician bowed himself to the earth, dug his fingers in the sand, and drew forth a handful of ducats, which he threw into the boy's cap.

'Thanks,' replied the youth; 'this money will be very useful

to my mother, but you must give me a better pledge than that. I must have a piece of your ear.'

'Will nothing else serve?'

'Nothing!'

'Well, then,' said the magician, 'take your knife.'

'I have no knife with me,' replied the youth; 'you must lend me yours.'

The magician obediently lent his knife, and bent his right ear towards the youth.

'No, no, I want the left ear; you offer the right far too willingly.'

The magician then offered his left ear; and the youth cut off a slant piece, laid it in his wallet, and then drew his stick out of the ground. The magician groaned, rubbed his mutilated ear, then, turning a somersault, changed himself into a black cock, ordered the youth to take his mother back, and return at midnight and await his arrival at the cross-road where they now stood, when he would take him home and teach him for three years. The cock then flapped his wings, changed into a magpie, and flew away.

When the youth had accompanied his mother to the next village he kissed her hands and feet, shook the gold into her apron, and begged her to call for him in three years at the place where he had made his agreement with the magician. He then hastened back and reached the cross-road just at midnight.

Being very tired he leaned against the milestone to await the arrival of his master. He waited long, then as no one came, he drew the piece of the magician's ear from his wallet and bit it hard. At this the milestone staggered, cracked, and roared. The youth sprang quickly aside, looked at the inscription, and cried: 'Ho! ho! Is that you, master?'

'Of course, it is! But why did you bite me?' asked the magician.

'Take human form instantly!' replied the youth.

'I have done so!' With this the man in black stood on the cross-road. 'Now we will go home,' said he. 'I take you as my pupil, but remember, from this moment you remain my pupil and servant, until, the three years ended, your mother fetches you away.'

Thus the youth became the magician's pupil. You wish to know how he taught him his art? Well, so be it. He stretched his hands and feet, turned him into a paper bag, and then left him to return to his proper shape as best he could. Or else, he thrust his hand and arm up to the shoulder down the youth's throat, turned him inside out, and left him to turn himself right.

The youth learnt so well, that at the end of the three years his skill in magic surpassed even that of his master. During this time many parents had come to fetch their children, for the magician had quite a crowd of pupils; but the cunning old man always contrived that they went away without them. Three days before the time appointed for the shoemaker's wife to fetch her son, the youth met her on the road and told her how to recognize him.

'Remember, dearest mother,' said he, 'when the magician calls his horses together, a fly will buzz over my ear; when the doves fly down, I shall not eat of the peas; and when the maidens stand around you, a brown mole will make its appearance above my eyebrow! Be sure you remember this, or you will destroy us both.'

When the shoemaker's wife demanded her son of the magician, he blew a brazen trumpet towards all four corners of the world. Immediately a crowd of coal-black horses rushed forward; they were not, however, real horses, but enchanted scholars.

'Find your son – then you can take him with you!' said the magician.

The mother went from horse to horse, trying hard to recognize her son; she trembled at the mere thought that she might make a mistake, and thus destroy both herself and her beloved child. At length she noted a fly buzzing over the ear of one of the horses, and cried joyfully: 'That is my son!'

'Right,' said the magician; 'now guess again.' So saying he blew a silver trumpet towards the corners of the earth, and threw on the ground half a bushel of peas. Then like some vast cloud down flew a flock of doves, and began eagerly picking up the peas. The shoemaker's wife looked at dove after dove, until she found one that only appeared to eat. 'That is my son!' said she.

'Right again! Now comes the third and last trial. Guess right, and your son goes with you; guess wrong, and he remains with me for ever.' The magician then blew his trumpet, and immediately beautiful songs resounded through the air. At the same time lovely maidens approached and surrounded the shoemaker's wife. They were all crowned with corn-flowers, and wore white robes with rose-coloured girdles.

The shoemaker's wife examined each carefully, and saw a brown mole over the right eye of the most beautiful. 'This is my son!' she exclaimed.

Scarcely had she spoken than the maiden changed into her son, threw himself into her arms, and thanked her for his deliverance. The other maidens flew away, and the mother and son returned home.

The student of magic had not been long at home before he discovered that in his father's house Want was a constant guest. The money given by the magician had long since come to an end, for the shoemaker had spent it all in drink.

'What have you learnt in foreign parts?' he asked his son. 'What help am I to expect from you?'

'I have learned magic, and will give you help enough. I can

at your wish change myself into all possible shapes, today into a falcon, tomorrow into a greyhound, a nightingale, a sheep, or any other form. Lead me as an animal to market, and there sell me, but be sure always to bring back the rope with which you led me thither, and never desire me to become a horse; the money thus acquired would be useless to you, and you would make me, and through me yourself, unhappy.'

Thereupon the shoemaker demanded a falcon for sale; his son at once disappeared, and a splendid falcon sat on the father's shoulder. The shoemaker took the bird to market, where he sold it to a hunter for a good price, but on returning home, he found his son seated at the table enjoying a good dinner.

When the money thus gained had been spent to the last farthing, the shoemaker required a greyhound, which he again sold to a hunter, and on his return home found his son had arrived there before him.

Thus the father led his son to market again and again, as an ox, a cow, a sheep, a goose, a turkey, and in many other animal forms. One day he thought: 'I should very much like to know why my son does not wish to become a horse! Surely he takes me for a fool, and grudges me the best prize!' He was half drunk when he thought this, and then and there desired his son to become a horse. Hardly had he spoken than his wish was gratified: a splendid horse stood before the window; he dug his hoofs deep into the ground, whilst his eyes shot forth lightning and flames issued from his nostrils.

The shoemaker mounted and rode into the town. Here a merchant stopped him, admired the horse, and offered to give the animal's weight in gold if his master would only sell him. They went together to a pair of scales: the merchant shook gold from a sack on one of the wooden scales, whilst the shoemaker made his horse mount on the other. As he was staring in amazement at the heap of gold in the scales, one of the chains broke, and the gold pieces rolled over the street. The shoemaker threw himself on the ground to pick them up, and forgot both the horse and bridle.

The merchant meanwhile mounted the horse, and galloped out of the town, digging his spurs into the poor animal's sides until the blood flowed, and beating him cruelly with a steel riding-whip; for this merchant was none other than the magician, who thus revenged himself for the piece cut from his ear.

The poor horse was quite exhausted when the magician arrived with him at his invisible dwelling; this house, it is true, stood in an open field, yet no one could see it. The horse was then led to the stable, while the magician considered how he might best torture him.

But while the magician was considering, the horse, who knew what a terrible fate awaited him, succeeded in throwing the bridle over a nail, on which it remained hanging, thus enabling him to draw his head out. He fled across the field, and changing into a gold ring, threw himself before the feet of a beauteous Princess just returning from bathing.

The Princess stooped, picked up the gold circle, slipped it on her finger, and then looked around in wonder. In the meantime, the magician – changed into a Grecian merchant – came up and courteously asked the Princess to return the gold ring he had lost. Terrified at the sight of his black beard and gleaming eyes, the Princess screamed aloud, and pressed the ring to her breast.

Alarmed by her cries, her attendants and playmates, who were waiting near, hastened up and formed a circle round their beloved Princess. But as soon as they understood the cause of her distress, they threw themselves on the importunate stranger, and began tickling him in such a manner that he laughed, cried, giggled, coughed, and at length danced over the ground like a maniac, forgetting through sheer distress that he was still a magician.

When, however, he did remember it, he changed himself into a hedgehog, and stuck his bristles into the maidens until their blood flowed, and they were glad to leave him alone.

Meanwhile the Princess hastened home and showed her father the ring, which pleased her so much that she wore it on her heart-finger night and day. Once when playing with it, the ring slipped from her hand, fell to the ground and sprang in pieces, when, oh, wonder! before her stood a handsome youth, the magician's pupil.

At first the Princess was very troubled, and did not venture to raise her eyes, but when the scholar had told her everything she was satisfied, conversed with him a long while, and promised to ask her father to have the magician driven away by the dogs should he ever come to demand the ring. When in the course of the day the magician came, the King, in spite of all his daughter's entreaties, ordered the ring to be given up.

With tears in her eyes the Princess took the ring (the scholar had resumed this form immediately after relating his adventures) and threw it at the merchant's feet. It shivered into little pearls.

Trembling with rage, the merchant threw himself on the ground in the shape of a hen, picked up the pearls, and when he saw no more, flew out of the window, flapped his wings, cried, 'Kikeriki! Scholar, are you there?' and then soared into the air.

Having been told by the scholar what to do should she be compelled to return the ring, the Princess had let her hand-kerchief fall at the same moment she threw the ring on the ground, and two of the largest pearls had rolled beneath it. She now took out these pearls, and they immediately called, in mocking imitation of the hen's voice:

'Kikeriki! I am here!'

They then changed into a hawk and chased after the hen. Seizing it with his sharp talons, he bit its left wing with such force that all the feathers cracked, and the hen fell like a stone into the water, where it was drowned.

The hawk then returned to the Princess, perched on her shoulder, gazed fondly into her eyes, and then became once more the young and handsome scholar. The Princess had grown so fond of him that she chose him as her husband, and from that moment he gave up magic for ever. In his prosperity he did not forget his relations – his mother lived with him and the Princess in their magnificent palace, his sisters married wealthy merchants, and even his father was content.

When the old King died the magician's pupil became King over the land, and lived so happily with his wife and children, and all his subjects, that no pen can write, no song sing, and no story tell of half their happiness.

The Magicians' Gifts

JULIANA HORATIA EWING

THERE was once a king in whose dominions lived no less than three magicians.

When the king's eldest son was christened, the king invited the three magicians to the christening feast, and to make the compliment the greater, he asked one of them to stand godfather. But the other two, who were not asked to be godfathers, were so angry at what they held to be a slight, that they only waited to see how they might best revenge themselves upon the infant prince.

When the moment came for presenting the christening gifts, the godfather magician advanced to the cradle and said, 'My gift is this: Whatever he wishes for he shall have. And only I who give shall be able to recall this gift.' For he perceived the jealousy of the other magicians, and knew that, if possible, they would undo what he did. But the second magician muttered in his beard, 'And yet I will change it to a curse.' And coming up to the cradle, he said, 'The wishes that he has thus obtained he shall not be able to revoke or change.'

Then the third magician grumbled beneath his black robe, 'If he were very wise and prudent he might yet be happy. But I will secure his punishment.' So he also drew near to the cradle, and said, 'For my part, I give him a hasty temper.'

After which the two dissatisfied magicians withdrew together, saying, 'Should we permit ourselves to be slighted for nothing?'

But the king and his courtiers were not at all disturbed.

'My son has only to be sure of what he wants,' said the king, 'and then, I suppose, he will not desire to recall his wishes.'

And the courtiers added, 'If a prince may not have a hasty temper, who may, we should like to know?'

And everybody laughed, except the godfather magician, who went out sighing and shaking his head, and was seen no more.

Whilst the king's son was yet a child, the gift of the godfather magician began to take effect. There was nothing so rare and precious that he could not obtain it, or so difficult that it could not be accomplished by his mere wish. But, on the other hand, no matter how inconsiderately he spoke, or how often he changed his mind, what he had once wished must remain as he had wished it, in spite of himself; and as he often wished for things that were bad for him, and oftener still wished for a thing one day and regretted it the next, his power was the source of quite as much pain as pleasure to him. Then his temper was so hot, that he was apt hastily to wish ill to those who offended him, and afterwards bitterly to regret the mischief that he could not undo. Thus one after another, the king appointed his trustiest counsellors to the charge of his son, who, sooner or later, in the discharge of their duty, were sure to be obliged to thwart him; on which the impatient prince would cry, 'I wish you were at the bottom of the sea with your rules and regulations'; and the counsellors disappeared accordingly, and returned no more.

When there was not a wise man left at court, and the king himself lived in daily dread of being the next victim, he said, 'Only one thing remains to be done; to find the godfather magician, and persuade him to withdraw his gift.'

So the king offered rewards, and sent out messengers in every direction, but the magician was not to be found. At last, one day he met a blind beggar, who said to him, 'Three nights ago I dreamed that I went by the narrowest of seven roads to seek what you are looking for, and was successful.

When the king returned home, he asked his courtiers,

'Where are there seven roads lying near to each other, some broad, and some narrow?' And one of them replied, 'Twenty-one miles to the west of the palace is a four-cross road, where three field-paths also diverge.'

To this place the king made his way, and taking the narrowest of the field-paths, went on and on till it led him straight into a cave, where an old woman sat over a fire.

'Does a magician live here?' asked the king.

'No one lives here but myself,' said the old woman. 'But as I am a wise woman I may be able to help you if you need it.'

The king then told her of his perplexities, and how he was desirous of finding the magician, to persuade him to recall his gift.

'He could not recall the other gifts,' said the wise woman. 'Therefore it is better that the prince should be taught to use his power prudently and to control his temper. And since all the persons capable of guiding him have disappeared, I will return with you and take charge of him myself. Over me he will have no power.'

To this the king consented, and they returned together to the palace, where the wise woman became guardian to the prince, and she fulfilled her duties so well that he became much more discreet and self-controlled. Only at times his violent temper got the better of him, and led him to wish what he afterwards vainly regretted.

Thus all went well till the prince became a man, when, though he had great affection for her, he felt ashamed of having an old woman for his counsellor, and he said, 'I certainly wish that I had a faithful and discreet adviser of my own age and sex.'

On that very day a young nobleman offered himself as companion to the prince, and as he was a young man of great ability, he was accepted; whereupon the old woman took her departure, and was never seen again.

The young nobleman performed his part so well that the prince became deeply attached to him, and submitted in every way to his counsels. But at last a day came when, being in a rage, the advice of his friend irritated him, and he cried hastily, 'Will you drive me mad with your long sermons? I wish you would hold your tongue for ever.' On which the young nobleman became dumb, and so remained. For he was not, as the wise woman had been, independent of the prince's power.

The prince's grief and remorse knew no bounds. 'Am I not under a curse?' said he. 'Truly I ought to be cast out from human society, and sent to live with wild beasts in a wilderness. I only bring evil upon those I love best – indeed, there is no hope for me unless I can find my godfather, and make him recall this fatal gift.'

So the prince mounted his horse, and, accompanied by his dumb friend, who still remained faithful to him, he set forth to find the magician. They took no followers, except the prince's dog, a noble hound, who was so quick of hearing that he understood all that was said to him, and was, next to the young nobleman, the wisest person at court.

'Mark well, my dog,' said the prince to him, 'we stay nowhere till we find my godfather, and when we find him we go no further. I rely on your sagacity to help us.'

The dog licked the prince's hand, and then trotted so resolutely down a certain road that the two friends allowed him to lead them and followed close behind.

They travelled in this way to the edge of the king's dominions, only halting for needful rest and refreshment. At last the dog led them through a wood, and towards evening they found themselves in the depths of the forest, with no sign of any shelter for the night. Presently they heard a little bell, such as is rung for prayer, and the dog ran down a side path and led them straight to a kind of grotto, at the door of which stood an aged hermit.

'Does a magician live here?' asked the prince.

'No one lives here but myself,' said the hermit, 'but I am old, and have meditated much. My advice is at your service if you need it.'

The prince then related his history, and how he was now seeking the magician godfather, to rid himself of his gift.

'And yet that will not cure your temper,' said the hermit. 'It were better that you employed yourself in learning to control that, and to use your power prudently.'

'No, no,' replied the prince, 'I must find the magician.'

And when the hermit pressed his advice, he cried, 'Provoke me not, good father, or I may be base enough to wish you ill; and the evil I do I cannot undo.'

And he departed, followed by his friend, and calling his dog. But the dog seated himself at the hermit's feet and would not move. Again and again the prince called him, but he only whined and wagged his tail, and refused to move. Coaxing and scolding were both in vain, and when at last the prince tried to drag him off by force, the dog growled.

'Base brute!' cried the prince, flinging him from him in a transport of rage. 'How have I been so deceived in you? I wish you were hanged!' And even as he spoke the dog vanished, and as the prince turned his head he saw the poor beast's body dangling from a tree above him. The sight overwhelmed him, and he began bitterly to lament his cruelty.

'Will no one hang me also,' he cried, 'and rid the world of such a monster?'

'It is easier to die repenting than to live amending,' said the hermit; 'yet is the latter course the better one. Wherefore abide with me, my son, and learn in solitude those lessons of self-government without which no man is fit to rule others.'

'It is impossible,' said the prince. 'These fits of passion are as a madness that comes upon me, and they are beyond cure. It only remains to find my godfather, that he may make me less baneful to others by taking away the power I abuse.' And raising the body of the dog tenderly in his arms, he laid it before him on his horse, and rode away, the dumb nobleman following him.

They now entered the dominions of another king, and in due time arrived at the capital. The prince presented himself to the king, and asked if he had a magician in his kingdom.

'Not to my knowledge,' replied the king. 'But I have a remarkably wise daughter, and if you want counsel she may be able to help you.'

The princess accordingly was sent for, and she was so beautiful, as well as witty, that the prince fell in love with her, and begged the king to give her to him to wife. The king, of course, was unable to refuse what the prince wished, and the wedding was celebrated without delay; and by the advice of his wife the prince placed the body of his faithful dog in a glass coffin, and kept it near him, that he might constantly be reminded of the evil results of giving way to his anger.

For a time all went well. At first the prince never said a harsh word to his wife; but by and by familiarity made him less careful, and one day she said something that offended him, and he fell into a violent rage. As he went storming up and down, the princess wrung her hands, and cried, 'Ah, my dear husband, I beg of you be careful what you say to me. You say you loved your dog, and yet you know where he lies.'

'I know that I wish you were with him, with your prating!' cried the prince, in a fury; and the words were scarcely out of his mouth when the princess vanished from his side, and when he ran to the glass coffin, there she lay, pale and lifeless, with her head upon the body of the hound.

The prince was now beside himself with remorse and misery, and when the dumb nobleman made signs that they should pursue their search for the magician, he only cried, 'Too late! too late!'

But after a while he said, 'I will return to the hermit, and pass the rest of my miserable life in solitude and penance. And you, dear friend, go back to my father.'

But the dumb nobleman shook his head, and could not be persuaded to leave the prince. Then they took the glass coffin on their shoulders, and on foot, and weeping as they went, they retraced their steps to the forest.

For some time the prince remained with the hermit, and submitted himself to his direction. Then the hermit bade him return to his father, and he obeyed.

Every day the prince stood by the glass coffin, and beat his breast and cried, 'Behold, murderer, the fruits of anger!' And he tried hard to overcome the violence of his temper. When he lost heart he remembered a saying of the hermit: 'Patience had far to go, but she was crowned at last.' And after a while the prince became as gentle as he had before been violent. And the king and all the court rejoiced at the change; but the prince remained sad at heart, thinking of the princess.

One day he was sitting alone, when a man approached him, dressed in a long black robe.

'Good-day, godson,' said he.

'Who calls me godson?' said the prince.

'The magician you have so long sought,' said the god-father. 'I have come to reclaim my gift.'

'What cruelty led you to bestow it upon me?' asked the prince.

'The king, your father, would have been dissatisfied with any ordinary present from me,' said the magician, 'forgetting that the responsibilities of common gifts, and very limited power, are more than enough for most men to deal with. But I have not neglected you. I was the wise woman who brought you up. Again, I was the hermit, as your dog was sage enough to discover. I am come now to reclaim what has caused you such suffering.'

'Alas!' cried the prince, 'why is your kindness so tardy? If you have not forgotten me, why have you withheld this benefit till it is too late for my happiness? My friend is dumb, my wife is dead, my dog is hanged. When wishes cannot reach these, do you think it matters to me what I may command?'

'Softly, prince,' said the magician; 'I had a reason for the delay. But for these bitter lessons you would still be the slave of the violent temper which you have conquered, and which, as it was no gift of mine, I could not remove. Moreover, when the spell which made all things bend to your wish is taken away, its effects also are undone. Godson! I recall my gift.'

As the magician spoke the glass sides of the coffin melted into the air, and the princess sprang up, and threw herself into her husband's arms. The dog also rose, stretched himself, and wagged his tail. The dumb nobleman ran to tell the good news to the king, and all the counsellors came back in a long train from the bottom of the sea, and set about the affairs of state as if nothing had happened.

The old king welcomed his children with open arms, and they all lived happily to the end of their days.

The Magician Turned Mischief-maker

JULIANA HORATIA EWING

THERE was once a wicked magician who prospered, and did much evil for many years. But there came a day when Vengeance, disguised as a blind beggar, overtook him, and outwitted him, and stole his magic wand. With this he had been accustomed to turn those who offended him into any shape he pleased; and now that he had lost it he could only transform himself.

As Vengeance was returning to his place, he passed through a village, the inhabitants of which had formerly lived in great terror of the magician, and told them of the downfall of his power. But they only said, 'Blind beggars have long tongues. One must not believe all one hears,' and shrugged their shoulders and left him.

Then Vengeance waved the wand and said, 'As you have doubted me, distress each other!' and so departed.

By and by he came to another village, and told the news. But here the villagers were full of delight, and made a feast, and put the blind beggar in the place of honour; who, when he departed, said, 'As you have done by me, deal with each other always!' and went on to the next village.

In this place he was received with even warmer welcome; and when the feast was over, the people brought him to the bridge which led out of the village, and gave him a guide-dog to help him on his way.

Then the blind beggar waved the wand once more and said:

'Those who are so good to strangers must needs be good to each other. But that nothing may be wanting to the peace of

this place, I grant to the beasts and birds in it that they may understand the language of men.'

Then he broke the wand in pieces, and threw it into the stream. And when the people turned their heads back again from watching the bits as they floated away, the blind beggar was gone.

Meanwhile the magician was wild with rage at the loss of his wand, for all his pleasure was to do harm and hurt. But when he came to himself he said: 'One can do a good deal of harm with his tongue. I will turn mischief-maker; and when the place is too hot to hold me, I can escape in what form I please.'

Then he came to the first village, where Vengeance had gone before, and here he lived for a year and a day in various disguises; and he made more misery with his tongue than he had ever accomplished in any other year with his magic wand. For everyone distrusted his neighbour, and was ready to believe ill of him. So parents disowned their children, and husbands and wives parted, and lovers broke faith; and servants and masters disagreed; and old friends became bitter enemies, till at last the place was intolerable even to the magician, and he changed himself into a cockchafer, and flew to the next village, where Vengeance had gone before.

Here also he dwelt for a year and a day, and then he left it because he could do no harm. For those who loved each other trusted each other, and the magician made mischief in vain. In one of his disguises he was detected, and only escaped with his life from the enraged villagers by changing himself into a cockchafer and flying on to the next place, where Vengeance had gone before.

In this village he made less mischief than in the first, and more than in the second. And he exercised all his art, and changed his disguises constantly; but the dogs knew him under all.

One dog – the oldest dog in the place – was keeping watch over the miller's house: when he saw the magician approaching, in the disguise of an old woman.

'Do you see that old witch?' said he to the sparrows, who were picking up stray bits of grain in the yard. 'With her evil tongue she is parting my master's daughter and the finest young fellow in the country-side. She puts lies and truth together, with more skill than you patch moss and feathers to build nests. And when she is asked where she heard this or that, she says, "A little bird told me so!"'

'We never told her,' said the sparrows indignantly, 'and if we had your strength, Master Keeper, she should not malign us long!'

'I believe you are right!' said Master Keeper. 'Of what avail is it that we have learned the language of men, if we do not help them to the utmost of our powers? She shall torment my young mistress no more.'

Saying which he flew upon the disguised magician as he entered the gate, and would have torn him limb from limb, but that the mischief-maker changed himself as before into a cockchafer, and flew hastily from the village.

And thus he might doubtless have escaped to do yet further harm, had not three cock-sparrows overtaken him just before he crossed the bridge.

From three sides they hemmed him in, crying, 'Which of us told you?' 'Which of us told you?' 'Which of us told you?' – and pecked him to pieces before he could transform himself again.

After which peace and prosperity befell all the neighbourhood.

The Princess and the Cat

E. NESBIT

THE day when everything began to happen to the Princess began just like all her ordinary days. The sun was shining, the birds were singing, and the Princess jumped out of bed and ran into the nursery to let the mice out of the traps in the nursery cupboard. The traps were set every night with a little bit of cheese in each, and every morning nurse found that not a single trap had caught a single mouse. This was because the Princess always let them go. No one knew this except the Princess and, of course, the mice themselves. And the mice never forgot it.

Then came bath and breakfast, and then the Princess ran to the open window and threw out the crumbs to the birds that flew down fluttering and chirping into the marble terrace. Before lessons began she had an hour for playing in the garden. But she never began to play till she had been round to see if any rabbits or moles were caught in the traps the palace gardeners set. The gardeners were lazy, and seldom got to work before half-past eight, so she always had plenty of time for this.

Then came lessons with dear old Professor Ouatidont-noisuntwuthnoing, and then more play, and dinner, and needlework, and play again.

And now it was teatime.

'Eat up your bread-and-butter, Your Highness,' said nurse, 'and then you shall have some nice plummy cake.'

'I don't feel plum-cakey at all today, somehow,' said the Princess. 'I feel just exactly as if something was going to happen.'

'Something's always happening,' said nurse.

'Ah! but I mean something horrid,' said the Princess. 'I expect uncle's going to make some nasty new law about me. Last time it was: "The Princess is only to wear a white frock on the first Sunday in the month." He said it was economy, but I know it was only spite.'

'You mustn't say that, dear,' said nurse. 'You know your rosy and bluey frocks are just as pretty as the white'; but in her heart she agreed with the Princess Everilda.

The Princess's father and mother had died when she was quite little, and her uncle was Regent. Now, you will have noticed that there is something about uncles which makes it impossible for them to be good in fairy stories. So of course this uncle was bad, as bad as he could be, and everyone hated him.

In fact, though it was now, as I have said, everybody's tea-time, nobody was making any tea: instead they were making a revolution. And just as the Princess was looking at the half-moon-shaped hole left by her first bite into her first piece of bread-and-butter, the good Professor burst into the nursery with his great grey wig all on one side, crying out in a very loud and very choky voice:

'The revolution! It's come at last. I knew the people would never stand that last tax on soap.'

'The Princess!' said nurse, turning very pale.

'Yes, I know,' said the Professor. 'There's a boat on the canal, blue sails with gold letters "P.P." – Pupil of the Professor. It's waiting. You go down there at once. I'll take the Princess out down the back stairs.'

He caught the Princess by her pink bread-and-buttery hand, and dragged her away.

'Hurry, my dear,' he panted; 'it's as much as your life is worth to delay a minute.'

But he himself delayed quite three minutes, and that was

one minute too long. He had just run into the palace library for the manuscript of his life's work, 'Everything Easily Explained', when the revolutionary crowd burst in, shouting 'Liberty and Soap!' and caught him. They did not see the Princess Everilda, because he had just time, when he heard them coming, to throw a red and green crochet antimacassar over her, and to hide her behind an armchair.

'When they've taken me away, go down the back stairs, and try to find the boat,' he whispered, just before they came and took him away.

And then Everilda was left alone. When everything was quiet, she said to herself: 'Now, you mustn't cry; you must do as you're told.' And she went down the palace back stairs, and out through the palace kitchen into the street.

She had never set foot in the streets before, but she had been driven through them in a coach with four white horses, and she knew the way to the canal.

The canal boat with the blue sails was waiting, and she would have got to it safely enough, but she heard a rattling sound, and when she looked she saw two boys tying an old rusty kettle to a cat's tail.

'You horrid boys!' she said; 'let poor pussy alone.'

'Not us,' said the boys.

Everilda instantly slapped them both, and they were so surprised that they let the cat go. It scuttled and scurried off, and so did the Princess. The boys threw stones after her and also after the cat, but fortunately they were both very bad shots and nobody was hit.

Even then the Princess would have got safely away, but she saw a boy sitting on a doorstep crying. So she stopped to ask what was the matter.

'I'm hungry,' said the boy, 'and father and mother are dead, and my uncle beat me, so I'm running away –'

'Oh,' said the Princess, 'so am I. What fun! And I've got

a horrid uncle too. You come with me, and we'll find my
nurse. *She's* running away, too. Make haste, or it'll be too
late.'

But when they got to the corner, it *was* too late.

The revolutionary crowd caught them; they shouted
'Liberty and Soap!' and they sent the boy to the workhouse,
and they put the Princess in prison; and a good many of them
wanted to cut off her pretty little head then and there, because
they thought she would be sure to grow up horrid like her
uncle the Regent.

But all the people who had ever been inside the palace said
what a nice little girl the Princess really was, and wouldn't
hear of cutting off her darling head. So at last it was decided
to get rid of her by enchantment, and the Head Magician to
the Provisional Revolutionary Government was sent for.

'Certainly, citizens,' he said, 'I'll put her in a tower on the
Forlorn Island, in the middle of the Perilous Sea – a nice strong
tower, with only one way out.'

'That's one too many. There's not to be any way out,' said
the people.

'Well, there's a way out of everything, you know,' said the
Magician timidly – he was trembling for his own head – 'but
it's fifty thousand millions to one against her ever finding it.'

So they had to be content with that, and they fetched
Everilda out of her prison; and the Magician took her hand
and called his carriage, which was an invention of his own –
half dragon, and half motor-car, and half flying-machine – so
that it was a carriage and a half, and came when it was called,
tame as any pet dog.

He lifted Everilda in, and said 'Gee up!' to his patent
carriage, and the intelligent creature geed up right into the air
and flew away. The Princess shut her eyes tight, and tried not
to scream. She succeeded.

When the Magician's carriage got to the place where it

knew it ought to stop, it did stop, and tumbled Everilda out on to a hard floor, and went back to its master, who patted it, and gave it a good feed of oil, and fire, and water, and petroleum spirit.

The Princess opened her eyes as the sound of the rattling dragon wings died away. She was alone – quite alone. 'I won't stay here,' said Everilda; 'I'll run away again.'

She ran to the edge of the tower and looked down. The tower was in the middle of a garden, and the garden was in the middle of a wood, and the wood was in the middle of a field, and after the field there was nothing more at all except steep cliffs and the great rolling, raging waves of the Perilous Sea.

'There's no way to run away by,' she said; and then she remembered that even if she ran away, there was now no-where to run to, because the people had taken her palace away from her, and the palace was the only home she had ever had – and where her nurse was goodness only knew.

'So I suppose I've got to live here till someone fetches me,' she said, and stopped crying, like a brave King's daughter as she was.

'I'll explore,' said Everilda all alone; 'that will be fun.' She said it bravely, and really it was more fun than she expected. The tower had only one room on each floor. The top floor was Everilda's bedroom; she knew that by her gold-backed brushes and things with 'E.P.' on them that lay on the toilet-table. The next floor was a sitting-room, and the next a dining-room, and the last of all was a kitchen, with rows of bright pots and pans, and everything that a cook can possibly want.

'Now I can play at cooking,' said the Princess. 'I've always wanted to do that. If only there was something to cook!'

She looked in the cupboards, and there were lots of canisters and jars, with rice, and flour, and beans, and peas, and lentils, and macaroni, and currants, and raisins, and candied peel, and sugar, and sago, and cinnamon. She ate a whole lump of candied citron, and enjoyed it very much.

'I shan't starve, anyway,' she said. 'But oh! of course, I shall soon eat up all these things, and then –'

In her agitation she dropped the jar; it did not break, but all the candied peel rolled away into corners and under tables. Yet when she picked the jar up it was as full as ever.

'Oh, hooray!' cried Everilda, who had once heard a sentry use that low expression; 'of course it's a magic tower, and everything is magic in it. The jars will always be full.'

The fire was laid, so she lighted it and boiled some rice, but it stuck to the pot and got burned. You know how nasty burned rice is? and the macaroni she tried to cook would not get soft. So she went out into the garden, and had a very much nicer dinner than she could ever have cooked. Instead of meat she had apples, and instead of vegetables she had plums, and she had peaches instead of pudding.

There were rows and rows of beautiful books in the sitting-

room, and she read a little, and wrote a long letter to nurse, in case anyone ever came who knew nurse's address and would post it for her. And then she had a nectarine-and-mulberry tea.

By this time the sun was sinking all red and splendid beyond the dark waters of the Perilous Sea, and Everilda sat down on the window seat to watch it.

I shall not tell you whether she cried at all then. Perhaps you would have cried just a little if you had been in her place.

'Oh dear! oh dear! oh dear!' she said, sniffing slightly. (Perhaps she had a cold.) 'There's nobody to tuck me up in bed – nobody at all.'

And just as she said it something fat and furry flew between her and the sunset. It hovered clumsily a moment and then swooped in at the window.

'Oh!' cried the Princess, very much frightened indeed.

'Don't you know me?' said the stout furry creature, folding its wings. 'I'm the cat you saved from the indignity of a rusty kettle in connection with my honourable tail.'

'But that cat hadn't got wings,' said Everilda, 'and you're much bigger than it, and it couldn't talk.'

'How do you know it couldn't talk,' said the Cat; 'did you ask it?'

'No,' said the Princess.

'Well, then!' said the Cat. 'And as for wings, I needn't wear them if you'd rather I didn't.'

The Cat took off her wings, rolled them neatly up, like your father rolls his umbrella, tied them round with a piece of string, and put them in the left-hand corner drawer in the bureau.

'That's better,' said Everilda.

'And as for size,' said the Cat, 'if I stayed ordinary cat-size I shouldn't be any use to you. And I've come to be cook, companion, house-maid, nurse, professor, and everything else, so –'

'Oh, don't,' said the Princess – '*don't* get any bigger.'

For while she was speaking the Cat had been growing steadily, and she was now about the size of a large leopard.

'Certainly not,' said the Cat obligingly; 'I'll stop at once.'

'I suppose', said the Princess timidly, 'that you're magic?'

'Of course,' said the Cat; 'everything is, here. Don't you be afraid of me, now! Come along, my pet, time for bed.'

Everilda jumped, for the voice was the voice of her nurse; but it was also the voice of the Cat.

'Oh!' cried the Princess, throwing her arms round the Cat's large furry neck, 'I'm not afraid of *any* thing when you speak like that.'

So, after all, she had someone to tuck her up in bed. The Cat did it with large, soft, furry, clever paws, and in two minutes Everilda was fast asleep.

And now began the long, lonely, but all the same quite happy time which the Princess and the Cat spent together on the Forlorn Island.

Everilda had lessons with the Cat – and then it was the Professor's voice that the Cat spoke with; and the two did the neat little housework of the tower together – and then the Cat's voice was like the voices of the palace house-maids. And they did the cooking and then the Cat's voice was the cook's voice. And they played games together – and then the voice of the Cat was like the voices of all sorts of merry children. It was impossible to be dull with a companion who changed so often.

'But who are you really?' the Princess used to ask.

And the Cat always answered:

'I give it up! Ask another!' as if the Princess had been playing at riddles.

'How is it our garden is always so tidy and full of nice fruit and vegetables?' the Princess asked once, when they had been on the island about a year.

'Oh,' said the Cat, 'didn't you know? The moles you used to let out of the traps do the digging, and the birds you used to feed bring the seeds in their little beaks, and the mice you used to save from the palace mouse-traps do the weeding and raking with their sharp little teeth, and their fine, neat, needly claws.'

'But how did they get here?' asked the Princess.

'The usual way – swimming and flying,' said the Cat.

'But aren't the mice afraid of *you*?'

'Of me?' The great Cat drew herself up to her full height. 'Anyone would think, to hear you, that I was a *common* cat.' And she was really cross for nearly an hour.

That was the only approach to a quarrel that the two ever had.

Sometimes, at first, the Princess used to say:

'How long am I to stay here, pussy-nurse?'

And the Cat always said in nurse's voice:

'Till you're grown up, my dear.'

And the years went by, and each year found the Princess more good, and clever, and beautiful. And at last she was quite grown up.

'Now,' said the Cat briskly, 'we must get to work. There's a Prince in a kingdom a long way off, and he's the only person who can get you off this island.'

'Does he know?' asked Everilda.

'He knows about *you*, but he doesn't know that he's the person to find you, and he doesn't know where you are. So now every night I must fly away and whisper about you in his ear. He'll think it's dreams, but he believes in dreams; and he'll come in a grand ship with masts of gold and sails of silk, and carry my Pretty away and make a Queen of her.'

'Shall I like that, pussy-nurse, do you think?' asked the Princess.

And the Cat replied:

'Yes, very much indeed. But you wouldn't like it if it were any other King than this one, so it's just as well that it's quite impossible for it to *be* any other.'

'How will he come?' asked the Princess.

'Don't I tell you? In a ship, of course,' said the Cat.

'Aren't the rocks dangerous?' asked the Princess.

'Oh, very,' the Cat answered.

'Oh,' said the Princess, and grew silent and thoughtful.

That night the Cat got out its rolled-up wings, and unrolled them, and brushed them, and fitted them on; then she lighted a large lamp and set it in the window that looked out on the Perilous Sea.

'That's the beacon to guide the King to you,' she said.

'Won't it guide other ships here?' asked the Princess, 'with perhaps the wrong Kings on board – the ones I shouldn't like being Queen with?'

'Very likely,' said the Cat; 'but it doesn't matter: they'd only be wrecked. Serve them right, coming after Princesses that don't want them.'

'Oh,' said Everilda.

The Cat spread her wings, and after one or two trial flights round the tower, she spread them very wide indeed, and flew away across the black Perilous Sea, towards a little half moon that was standing on its head to show sailors that there would be foul weather.

The Princess leaned her elbows on the window-sill and looked out over the sea. Down below in the garden she could hear the kind moles digging industriously, and the good little mice weeding and raking with their sharp teeth and their fine needly claws. And far away against the low-hanging moon she saw the sails and masts of a ship.

'Oh,' she cried, 'I *can't*! It's sure not to be *his* ship. It mustn't be wrecked.'

And she turned the lamp out. And then she cried a little,

because perhaps after all it might be his ship, and he would pass by and never know.

Next night the Cat went out on another flying excursion, leaving the lamp lighted. And again the Princess could not bear to go to bed leaving a lamp burning that might lure honest Kings and brave mariners to shipwreck, so she put out the lamp and cried a little. And this happened for many, many, many nights.

When the Cat swept the room of a morning she used to wonder where all the pearls came from that she found lying all about the floor. But it was a magic place, and one soon ceased to wonder much about anything. She never guessed that the pearls were the tears the Princess shed when she had put out the lamp, and seen ship after ship that perhaps carried her own King go sailing safely and ignorantly by, no one on board guessing that on that rock was a pretty, dear Princess waiting to be rescued – *the* Princess, the only Princess that that King would be happy and glad to have for his Queen.

And the years went on and on. Every night the Cat lighted the lamp and flew away to whisper dreams into the ears of the only King who could rescue the Princess, and every night the Princess put out the lamp and cried in the dark. And every morning the Cat swept up a dustpan full of pearls that were Everilda's tears. And again and again the King would fit out a vessel and sail the seas, and look in vain for the bright light that he had dreamed should guide him to his Princess.

The Cat was a good deal vexed; she could not understand how any King could be so stupid. She always stayed out all night. She used to go and see her friends after she had done whispering dreams to the King, and only got home in time to light the fire for breakfast, so she never knew how the Princess put out the lamp every night, and cried in the dark.

The years went by and went by, and the Princess grew old and grey, for she had never had the heart to leave the lamp alight, for fear that some poor mariners who were not her King should be drawn by the lamp to those cruel rocks and wrecked on them, for of course it wouldn't and couldn't be the poor mariners' fault that they didn't happen to be the one and only King who could land safely on the Forlorn Island.

And when the Princess was quite old, and the tear pearls that had been swept up by the Cat filled seven big chests in the back-kitchen, the Princess fell ill.

'I think I am going to die,' she said to the Cat, 'and I am not really at all sorry except for you. I think you'll miss me. Tell me now – it's almost all over – who are you, really?'

'I give it up,' said the Cat as usual. 'Ask another.'

But the Princess asked nothing more. She lay on her bed in her white gown and waited for death, for she was very tired of being alive. Only she said:

'Put out that lamp in the window; it hurts my eyes.'

For even then she thought of the poor men whose ships might be wrecked just because they didn't happen to be the one and only King with whom she could be happy.

So the Cat took the lamp away, but she did not put it out; she set it in the window of the parlour, and its light shone out over the black waters of the Perilous Sea.

And that very night the one and only King – who in all these years had never ceased to follow the leading of the dreams the Cat whispered in his ear – came in the black darkness sailing over the Perilous Sea. And in the black darkness he saw at last the bright white light that his dreams had promised, and he knew that where the light was his Princess was, and his heart leaped up, and he bade the helmsman steer for the light.

And for the light they steered. And because he was the only possible King to mate that Princess, the helmsman found the only possible passage among the rocks, and the ship anchored safely in a little quiet creek, and the King landed and went up to the door of the tower and knocked.

'Who's there?' said the Cat.

'Me,' said the King, just as you or I might have done.

'You're late,' said the Cat. 'I'm afraid you've lost your chance.'

'I took the first chance I got,' said the King. 'Let me in, and let me see her.'

He had been so busy all these years trying to find the bright white light of his dreams that he had not noticed that his hair had gone grey long ago.

So the Cat let him in, and led him up the winding stair to the room where the Princess, very quiet, lay on her white bed waiting for death to come, for she was very tired.

The old King stumbled across the bar of moonlight on the floor, flung down a clanking wallet, and knelt by the bed in the deep shadow, saying:

'Oh, my dear own Princess, I have come at last.'

'Is it really you?' she said, and gave him her hands in the shadow. 'I hoped it was Death's footstep I heard coming up the winding stair.'

'Oh, did you hope for death,' he cried, 'while I was coming to you?'

'You were long in coming,' said she, 'and I was very tired.'

'My beautiful dear Princess,' he said, 'you shall rest in my arms till you are not tired any more.'

'My beautiful King,' she said, 'I am not tired any more now.'

And then the Cat came in with the lamp, and they looked in each other's eyes.

Instead of the beautiful Princess of his dreams the King saw a white, withered woman whose piteous eyes met his in a look of longing love. The Princess saw a bent, white-haired man, but love was in his eyes.

'*I* don't mind.'

'*I* don't mind.

They both spoke together. And both thought they spoke the truth. But the truth was that both were horribly disappointed.

'Yet, all the same,' said the King to himself, 'old and withered as she is, she is more to me than the youngest and loveliest of all other Princesses.'

'I don't care if he *is* grey,' said the Princess to herself; 'whatever he is, he's the only possible one.'

'Here's a pretty kettle of fish!' said the Cat. 'Why on earth didn't you come before?'

'I came as soon as I could,' said the King.

The Cat, walking about the room in an agitated way, kicked against the wallet the King had dropped.

'What's this?' she said crossly, rubbing her toes, for the wallet was hard, and she had hurt herself more than a little.

'Oh, that,' said the King – 'that's just the steel bolts and hammers and things that my resolves to find the Princess turned into when I failed and never did find her. I never could bear to throw them away; I had a sort of feeling that they might be good for something, since they hurt me so much when they came to me. I thought perhaps I could batter down the doors of the Princess's tower with them.'

'They're good for something better than that,' said the Cat joyously.

She went away, and the two heard her hammering away below. Presently she staggered in with a great basket of white powder, and emptied it on the floor; then she went away for more.

The King helped her with the next basketful, and the next, and the next, and the next, and the next, and the next, for there were seven of them, and the heap of white powder stood up in the room as high as the King's middle.

'That's powder of pearls,' said the Cat proudly. 'Now, tell me, have you been a good King?'

'I have tried to be,' said the white-haired King. 'I was a workhouse boy, and then I was apprenticed to a magician who taught me how to make people happy. There was a revolution just at the time when I was put into the workhouse, and they had a Republic. And I worked my way up till they made me President.'

'What became of the King in that revolution?'

'There wasn't a King, only a Regent. They had him taught a trade, and he worked for his living. It was the worst punishment they could invent for him. There was a Princess, too, but she was hidden by a magician. I saw her once when she was trying to run away. She asked me to run too – to her nurse –'

Here his eyes met the Princess's.

'Oh,' she said, 'that was you, was it?'

'Oh,' said he, 'then that was you!'

And they looked long and lovingly in each other's faded eyes.

'Hurry up,' said the Cat impatiently; 'you were made President. And then –'

'Oh, why, then,' said the King, 'they thought it wouldn't be any more dangerous or expensive to have a King than a President, and prettier at State shows – ermine, crown, and sceptre, and all that – prettier than frock-coat and spats. So I agreed.'

'And do your people love you?' the Cat asked.

'I don't know,' said the King simply; 'I love them –'

As he spoke there came a flutter and flicker of many thousand wings at the closed casement. The Cat threw the window wide, and in swarmed a countless crowd of white pigeons.

'These are the blessings of your people,' said the Cat.

The wings fluttered and flickered and fanned the heap of

pearl dust on the floor till it burst into flame, and the flame rose up high and white and clear.

'Quick!' cried the Cat, 'walk through it. Lead her through.'

The old King gave his hand to his poor faded love, and raised her from her couch, and together they passed through the clear fire made of her patience and self-sacrifice, his high resolve, and the blessings of his people. And they came out of that fire on the other side.

'Oh, love, how beautiful you are!' cried the King.

'Oh, my King, your face is the face of all my dreams!' cried the Princess.

And they put their arms round each other and cried for joy, because now they were both young and beautiful again.

The Cat cried for sympathy.

'And now we shall live happily ever after,' said the Princess, putting her other arm round the Cat. 'Dear pussy-nurse, do tell me, now it's all over, who you really are.'

'I give it up. Ask another,' said the Cat.

But as she spoke she went herself through the fire, and on the other side came out – not one person, but eleven. She was, in fact, the Professor, the nurse, the palace butler, footman, housemaid, parlourmaid, between-maid, boots, scullion, boy in buttons, as well as the rescued cat – all rolled into one!

'But we only used one part of ourselves at a time,' they all said with one voice, 'and I hope we were useful.'

'You were a darling,' said the Princess – 'darlings, I mean. But who turned you all into exactly the pussy-nurse I wanted?'

'Oh, that was the Magician,' said all the voices in unison; 'he was your fairy-godfather, you know.'

'What has become of him?' asked the Princess, clinging to her lover's arm.

'He's been asleep all this time. It was the condition, the only way he got leave to work the good magic for all of us,' said the many voices that were one.

'Let's go and wake him,' said the King.

So they all went. And when they woke the Magician, who was sleeping quietly in his own private room in the palace where the Princess had once lived, he sneezed seven times for pure joy, and then called for Welsh rabbit and baked Spanish onions for supper.

'For after all these years of starvation,' he said, 'I do really think I may for once take a liberty with my digestion.'

So he had the supper he wanted; but the King and the Princess had roses and lilies and wedding-cake, because they were married that very evening.

And when you have passed through exactly the sort of fire those two had passed through, you can never be old, or ugly, or unhappy again, so those two are happy, and beautiful, and young to this very hour.

The Magician who Wanted More

ANDREW LANG

This is one of the stories which Andrew Lang, the collector of the Tales of the Coloured Fairy Books, tells us 'was made up altogether out of his own head by the Author, of course with the Historical Papers in the Kingdom of Pantouflia'. It is one of the 'Tales of a Fairy Court' which narrate some of the early adventures of Prince Prigio. In the story before this one, Prigio had an exciting adventure with a giant, which ended with the giant being reduced to normal size with the aid of Prigio's 'Wishing Cap', and returning to the Court of Pantouflia as his friend.

PRINCE PRIGIO had a kind heart, was very observant, and took notice of everybody. When the giant had been for a week or two at court, Prigio saw that though he was now no bigger than an ordinary tall man, and was very kindly treated by everybody, still he did not seem happy. The Prince was anxious to do his best for him, and took rides and walks with him, hoping that his friend would speak out, and tell his sorrow. But Monsieur von Hexenhausen (which was now the giant's title in society) was silent. One day they rode out with their favourite dogs, and with no companions. They had some food in their saddle-bags, and Prigio carried two bottles of the best champagne, one for himself and one for his friend; they meant to picnic beside some clear fountain in the forest. Fizzy, or effervescent, champagne had only been invented that year, and few people had even heard of it.

As they passed through the town, Hexenhausen looked up at the top of the church steeple, and sighed deeply. Prigio, too, looked and sighed, on the chance that his companion would think that the prince knew the cause of his melancholy.

This artifice succeeded.

'You know, I see,' said Hexenhausen, 'the cause of my inconsolable regret.'

Prigio had not a guess at it; his friend could not be inconsolable because he was no longer as tall as the steeple. He had become shorter by his own choice.

Prigio sighed again. 'There is a remedy for everything but death,' he said. 'You know that mine are no ordinary powers – can I not help you?'

'She is not *dead*,' said Hexenhausen. 'But how changed! You know the case, I see, though how you know I cannot guess.'

Prigio could not guess either. Who was 'she'? he wondered. So he shook his head wisely, and looked at Hexenhausen with a melancholy but not unhopeful smile. 'A cruel misfortune!' he said.

'Yes,' said Hexenhausen, dashing away a tear. 'In yonder glittering weathercock who but a husband could recognize his once beautiful and tender, and still beloved wife?'

'Who, indeed?' thought Prigio, much moved by the singularity of the circumstance. But he said, 'Enchantment, I suppose. What is the name of the wicked enchanter, that I may bring him to justice?'

Hexenhausen shook his head, and groaned. 'It is a most extraordinary thing,' he replied, 'or perhaps, when you come to think of it, it is not so very extraordinary after all, that, since I left off being a giant, my memory is no longer what it was. The change was so great and so rapid: my whole nature is altered, if you understand me. I *used* to know the name of the enchanter who turned my dear wife into the weathercock on the top of the steeple, because she would not listen to his prayers and desert me for him. But now I have forgotten. He is a very powerful magician. He has a wishing cap of his own, but even *that* could not overcome the fixed and loyal affection of my constant spouse. He took his revenge, as you see. There she is' (he waved his hand towards the now distant steeple) 'and here am I!'

'You neither know his name nor address?' said Prigio.

Hexenhausen shook his head. The prince, too, was silent, reflecting deeply, and they turned their horses into the forest. The prince was thinking how he could help his friend. He had none of his fairy presents with him; they were all at home, except the fairy watch, which was a very good one for ordinary purposes. At this moment the hounds, running about in the underwood and bracken, gave a cry, and Prigio saw the golden horns and white flanks of the fairy hind.

He uttered a view hollo, Hexenhausen blew his hunting-horn, and off they rode after the hounds, and the hounds after the deer, thinking about nothing but catching her.

'I seem to remember having seen a deer like that before,' said Hexenhausen, as they breathed their horses up a steep hill. 'It is like a dream. That is no common or forest deer. Oh, my poor memory,' and he passed his hand across his brow.

'I have read about a hind with golden horns in a book,' said Prigio; 'but I had no idea she was still running. There she goes, flashing through the brook. To her, Holdfast, to her, boy!' he shouted to his favourite hound.

'You have read all the books in the world,' said his friend admiringly, and setting spurs to their horses, they galloped down the slope, and through the ford.

Now that happened to Prigio which had happened to his father long ago. He was light, and had the swiftest of horses – a great-grandson of Cyclops (late the Eclipse colt) – while Monsieur von Hexenhausen was a very tall and heavy man. So Hexenhausen dropped back out of the chase, while on rode Prince Prigio, over seven bens, and even seven glens, and seven mountain moors, till he came to one of the four brown bounds of the sea.

Here Prigio at last drew rein, and looked about him. In

front was the great ocean, with never a sail on it, and all around was level grass-land, full of the finest cows and sheep that he had ever seen in his life, packed so close that you might wonder how they found food. The white hind had long been out of sight.

'Where in the world am I got to?' thought Prigio. 'My royal father's domains are not within a day's ride of the sea, yet certainly that is no mere lake.' Alighting from his weary horse, Prigio walked to the water and tasted it. 'Salt enough!' he said. 'I wonder what o'clock it is?'

He drew out his watch, the fairy time piece, which he had set that morning, at *Present Day*, and, lo, it marked *Fairy Times*.

'This is strange,' said Prigio to himself. 'If I am in fairy times, I must be in Fairyland, where anything may happen. A perilous adventure, truly! Would that I had my wishing cap, or even the sword of sharpness, or the cap of darkness, in case I meet with giants or enchanters. But, without the wishing cap there is no use in wishing. Prigio, my lad, all your magical things are far enough away, and you must rely on your own courage and natural acuteness.'

Looking around him, Prigio saw that though the rest of the land was a rich level plain, there arose, a mile away, a perpendicular black rock, as smooth as glass, with an enormous castle which covered all the top of it. There were hundreds of rooms piled high above till the topmost battlements were lost in the clouds. Taking his horse's bridle in his hand Prigio walked towards the rock. 'There must be some way of getting to the top,' he said to himself, 'though I don't see it.'

On he walked in his hunting boots across the sands, which were soft, and deep, and as black as coal.

At last he was beneath the cliff, which was so sheer that when he stood at the foot he could not see the castle, but he heard all the bells ringing a melancholy tune.

'There must be living people up there,' said Prigio, 'But how am I to get at them?'

The black wall of rock was as smooth as a window pane, with never a crack to set foot on. 'If I were a fly, I might climb it,' said Prigio, and at that moment a horrid thing happened. Down from the crest of the rock came creeping a common house fly, as large as a man. It crawled down till its odious eyes were on a level with Prigio's, and peered into his with a hungry look.

The prince leaped back and drew his hunting sword, but the fly merely beckoned to the right side with one of his monstrous feelers.

'I am to go round to the right?' said Prigio boldly.

The fly nodded, and, with a buzz like that of a thousand blue-bottles, flew up and out of sight.

'This is Fairyland, and no flies,' said the prince, using a vulgar and inappropriate form of speech, 'or rather, I wonder if they are *all* flies up there? Well, we shall see.'

So the prince walked round the rock to the right. It was as smooth as ever, but a golden nail with a large diamond head had been driven into it, and from the nail hung a beautiful ivory horn. Beside it, in letters of gold, were the words,

> Woe to the man who does not blow the horn,
> He shall have the shame and scorn.

On the other side was

> Woe to the man who does blow the horn,
> He may regret that ever he was born.

'Pretty bad verses, who ever made them,' said Prigio, 'and a pretty choice! But, whatever happens, I am not going to put up with shame and scorn.'

So he set the horn to his lips, and blew the notes of a tune which he liked,

My name it is little Jock Elliot,
And wha daur meddle wi' me!

The notes rang out clear and defiant. Then there was silence.

The prince knew that something out of the common was going to happen, and suddenly felt a pang of remorse. Since he and Hexenhausen had begun to talk under the steeple, Prigio had never once thought of his beautiful lady, who had never before been for ten minutes absent from his thoughts!

'Oh, Prigio!' the prince said to himself, 'false lover! Thou has forgotten her who is dearer to thee than thy life, her who in a few long weeks was to have been thy bride! Thou mayest never see her again, for who knows –'

At this moment there came a dreadful rushing noise, and an enormous winged dragon, all glittering in scales of blue, green, purple and gold, swept down from above, round the rock, swooped down on Prigio as a swallow swoops on a May fly, without a pause in its flight, and bore him up to the crest of the shining black cliff, and over the wall of bronze unbroken, which surrounds the castle. Here the dragon set Prigio down quite softly in a great green garden full of hundreds of the most beautiful ladies that ever were seen. Then the dragon soared with a shrill whoop to the loftiest battlement of the castle, where he disappeared.

Finding himself alone in the garden with white roses and red on every side, and with ladies as beautiful and as gaily dressed as the roses, Prigio naturally looked out for the prettiest of them. She was very tall, she had long flowing locks like gold, and she was dressed in white and red. Walking up to her, Prigio took off his hat with a sweeping bow, and knelt on one knee. 'Excuse, madam,' he said, 'the accidental trespass which has brought me, by no fault of my own, into your enchanted dominion. Permit me to name myself. I am Prigio, by men called Crown Prince of Pantouflia, and the humblest and most devoted of your servants.'

Then Prigio looked up at her with his great, soft brown eyes.

All the ladies came flocking together. Some were gold-haired and blue-eyed, and they wore white and red. Some were pale like white roses, and dark-haired, with large grey eyes, and they wore green silk and grey. Some were brown-haired, with rosy cheeks and blue eyes, and they wore brown and gold. Some had very fair hair and green eyes like emeralds, and they wore black and silver. Some had black eyes and black hair and they wore black and maize colour. Some had soft brown hair, and brown eyes, and they wore crimson velvet embroidered with gold. Some had dark blue eyes and dark hair, and they wore blue and peacock-coloured silk.

Prigio could not have counted the ladies. There were ladies all round him, fading away into the distance.

'Unhappy young prince,' said the first lady, 'are you a lover?'

Prigio felt that, if he had not been already engaged, he could have loved every one of them, and all of them at once, for they were like a garden of flowers, every one almost as pretty as all the others. But he knew that this was not a proper frame of mind, so he said, boldly, but sweetly, 'Madam, I am a true lover.'

'Then you shall make a good end,' said the lady, 'but alas for you, and alas for us, for you never can be ours!'

Then all the ladies sighed softly, as if a low sweet wind had passed over the roses.

'We are all princesses,' said the lady, 'stolen from all the kingdoms of fairyland by the most powerful and wicked of enchanters.'

Prigio thought, 'This must be the wretch who turned poor Hexenhausen's wife into a weathercock! Oh, how can I destroy his mischievous spells?'

The lady went on, 'He can turn himself into everything from a fly –'

'Madam, I met a rather large fly,' said the prince.

'To a dragon,' the lady went on.

'Madam, I was brought here by a rather fine dragon,' said the prince. 'May I ask the name of this magician?'

'He is called "The Magician who wants More",' said the lady. 'He has more sheep, cattle, gold, and wives, than all the kings in the world. He has everything but wine, which, for some reason, he is afraid to drink. But he will allow nobody to know his real name, because there is a prophecy that, if anyone knew his name, he would come to a bad end.'

'Is there no way of knowing his name, then?' asked the prince.

'None,' said the lady. 'When he is in good humour, we have all smiled on him, and asked his name: which, of course, is *our* name, by marriage, for we are all his wives, and it is very awkward for us not to know our own name. But he has only told his chief favourites bits of his name, little bits, and we cannot put them together.'

'Perhaps, if you told me, I might find out,' said the prince.

'We have tried that with other young men whom he has brought here,' said the lady, 'but they could never find the beginning or the end of it.'

'Still, there is no harm in trying,' said the prince.

'He told me', said the lady, 'that *gram* was part of it.'

'And me he told', said another lady, in green silk and grey, 'that *o* was part of it.'

'Perhaps an Irish name,' thought the prince, and, taking out his pocket-book, he wrote 'O'Gram'.

'And to me he said', whispered a lady in brown and gold, 'that *zer* was part of it.'

'O'Gramzer,' wrote the prince.

A lady in blue and silver said, '*Bub* is a bit of it.'

'O'Gramzerbub,' wrote the prince.

'*El* is part of it,' murmured a lady in black and maize colour.

'*El* sounds Hebrew,' said the prince. 'Let us try, *Elzero-grambub*, or *Bubelzerogram*, or *Gramobubelzer*.'

'There is another *el* in it,' said a lady in brown embroidered with gold.

'*Elelzerogrambub, Elbubelzerogram, Gramobubelzerel*,' tried the prince.

'Or stay,' said the prince, and, looking up, he saw the head of a huge man peeping at them over the battlements of the castle.

He guessed that this was the enchanter, and that the enchanter had been listening, so he did not say what he was going to have said. On the other hand he waved his hat and bowed to the enchanter, with a pleasant smile.

'Monsieur, I have guessed your secret,' he cried. 'You are Monsieur le Prince de Gramobubelzerel.'

'Clever fellow,' cried the enchanter. 'There is no deceiving *you*! Now come in, all of you, supper is waiting. *Mesdames sont servies!*' he added, in French, which, you know, means the same thing.

The prince gave his arm to the lady who had first spoken to him: all the rest followed in their companies, and they swept into the long hall which occupied the whole of the ground floor of the palace.

The enchanter received the prince with a bow: 'You will excuse my wearing my cap,' he said. 'It is a wishing cap, and saves us from the trouble of curious and clumsy servants. The dishes at a wish appear, and at a wish retire. Pray oblige me by taking the foot of the table.'

The prince bowed, and sat fronting the enchanter, who was hardly visible in the dim distance, so long was the hall. On one hand Prigio had the lady in rose white and rose red, on the left, a lady in green and grey. He made himself very agreeable, but his companions were sad.

'We don't think Gramobubelzerel *is* his real name,' said one of them. 'Another brave prince tried that before, and failed. For a week the palace rang with his shrieks: he died in extreme torment.'

Both ladies turned pale, and wiped away their tears.

'I'll take some more of that *salmis à la Marignan*, please,' said the prince to his empty dish, 'and asparagus, *à l'eau.*'

The dish flew away and came back with a helping.

'Excuse my barbarous appetite,' the prince went on to the lady, 'I have ridden since dawn, and had no luncheon. This is excellent milk,' he added, 'do you never have wine?'

'No, he is under a vow never to drink wine, because of a prophecy that it will be fatal to him.'

'A droll taste,' said the prince, 'may I drink your health in milk.'

They bowed to each other over their silver cups.

'It is brave of you to be hungry,' said the lady, 'but if you had heard these awful cries!'

'Courage, you shall hear no more of them,' said the prince, and presently, after the sweets, strawberries, and many sorts of ices, the ladies went to the drawing-room. The lady in white and red dropped her glove, which Prigio placed next his heart.

'Where *I* can never come!' said the pretty lady sadly to herself.

They were all in love with Prince Prigio.

The enchanter rose and, walking up the long hall, sat down beside the prince. 'Now,' he said, 'the ladies having gone, we may talk freely: may I ask your royal name?'

'Prigio, at your Grace's service, of Pantouflia.'

'Then I have the advantage of you, my name is not

Gramobubelzerel. It is the custom of the house that a visitor must guess my real name. If he does not, I shall not pain you by mentioning the consequences.'

'And if the visitor *does* know your name?' asked the prince, adding, 'by the way, after dinner in Pantouflia, we are accustomed to drink a kind of sweet, foaming liquid, that flows from a celebrated fountain, sparkling and fizzing, we call it "the well of singing water". I have here two flasks of it, will you join me in a glass?'

'Sparkling and fizzing?'

'Like the pool below a waterfall, or the sea behind a ship,' said Prigio.

'It cannot be *wine*, if it fizzes,' said the enchanter. 'Wine is flat stuff. I never touch it.'

Prigio produced his two flasks, drew a cork with a loud *cloop*, and poured three-quarters of the contents and more into a great silver cup, where it bubbled and sang, for the enchanter: the rest he poured into another cup for himself.

The prince then handed the giant the cup, saying, 'TE KUKLOPS, PIE OINON.'

'What's that? No good trying charms on *me*!' said the enchanter, whose classical education had been neglected.

He then took a sip. 'This is excellent water,' he said, 'sweet, cool, and pricks the palate in an agreeable way. Not like wine. But you were asking me, what happens if you know my name? I am not exactly aware of the consequences, but an ancient prophecy declared that I shall do something rather silly. I drink to your inclinations.

Prigo bowed, and drank.

'You may make three more guesses; upon my word that is a fine fountain of yours in Pantouflia! I never felt so happy!'

'Three more guesses?' said Prigio pensively.

'Yes, I drink to your royal father. Happily for him you have brothers.'

Here the enchanter greedily drank a pint of the champagne.

'Let me draw t'other flask,' said Prigio, and did so, pouring almost all of it into the enchanter's tall silver goblet.

'You are not Gramobubelzerel. Then are you Elelzero-grambub?'

'No. One guess gone,' said the enchanter, smiling horribly. 'I drink to my own luck, young man,' he went on very solemnly, 'If I did not know that you have had nothing but milk, I should shay that you are intosch, intoschiticated, thash t' shay, intoschcateted.'

Prigio saw that the unaccustomed beverage was getting about the wits of the enchanter.

'One guess gone!' said the prince. 'Now this must be right. Your highly respectable name is Elbubelzerogram.'

'Nonshenshe,' said the enchanter, swigging again. 'Two guesses gone. I never had such fun with any prince, since I began to be an enchanter.

> 'A jolly life is the Magic life,
>   A man does what he will,
>   He fears not sword, he fears not knife,
>   In his hall on the glassy hill.'

'*In his hall on the glassy hill,*' sang Prigio, by way of chorus.

'Made that poem myself,' said the enchanter sleepily, and he began to sing again, and beat the table with the handle of his fork.

'Music, the pipes!' he cried, and instantly the hall was full of the strains of a pibroch.

'Now, take your last shoot!' said the enchanter.

'My last guess?' said Prigio. 'Let me think. Your name is partly Hebrew, partly Greek!'

'No fishing questions!' said the enchanter.

'I have it! Your name', said Prigio, 'is Zerubabelelogram.'

An earthquake shook the glassy hill, and all the windows of crystal were shattered, all the chimneypots fell off, and all the ladies, who were listening behind the door, were heard to scream. The enchanter turned pale, and seizing his cup, drank off the last pint of the champagne. His colour returned, and his nose grew very red.

'Zerubabelelogram is himself again,' he cried.

'Prince, you are right, you are saved, but you have no more of that excellent fountain's water? What to do? I have it, come on!'

Saying these words the enchanter seized Prigio by the hand,

opened the door, scattered all the beautiful ladies, and dragged Prigio down a staircase.

The prince feared that he was being taken to the dungeon for torture, but down and down and *down*, the enchanter went.

'Open!' he cried to the wall, the wall opened and out rushed the enchanter to the shore of the sea. 'I want more,' he cried. 'More! I wish all the ocean to be that sweet, fizzy water.'

The sea began to foam and fizz, and, throwing off all his clothes, wishing cap and all, the enchanter rushed in, up to his knees, up to his waist, up to his chin, and began to drink. 'Rare!' he shouted. 'How delicious,' and fell to lapping again, while Prigio picked up the wishing cap and put it on.

'The prophecy was correct,' said the prince. 'This enchanter has done a silly thing. I wish him to go on drinking.'

The enchanter did go on drinking, singing, at intervals, that

'The magic life is a jolly life.'

Then his head began to flop on the waves; then his feet went up, and his head went down, then he turned and tried to swim, but his head went under, once, twice, thrice. It never came up again!

The enchanter, who always wanted more, had more than enough.

Prigio watched for some time, and had the curiosity to taste the ocean. It was champagne of the best quality.

Prigio then wished himself back among the ladies.

They all rushed to him, crying, 'Where is the enchanter?'

'Peace be on him!' said Prigio, very solemnly.

'Zerubabelelogram is gone to his account. Hush!' he cried as they all set up a shout of joy. 'It is ill boasting over dead enemies. You are free!'

They rushed on Prigio, and all, one after the other,

embraced and kissed their deliverer, with tears of joy, and of sorrow that he could never be theirs.

Prigio had the wishing cap on, and he might have wished them to leave off kissing him. But he thought that this was unworthy of a gentleman.

Afterwards he did not feel quite sure that he was right: so he wished that he might forget all about all of them, especially the lady in rose white and rose red, for Prigio was a true lover.

Then he wished them all home in their courts of Fairyland, and that they might all forget him, which they did, and made excellent marriages with handsome princes.

Disdaining to take the enchanter's treasures, Prigio wished them equally divided among the ladies, and then wished himself on his horse, at the foot of the church steeple of Pantouflia. There he found himself and, of course, he wished the weather-cock to be disenchanted. In a moment, the faithful and lovely wife of his friend, Hexenhausen, stood beside him, weeping tears of gratitude. Walking beside the lady, and leading his horse, Prigio passed through the long street to the gate of the royal park, where whom should he meet but Hexenhausen, leading home his wearied steed.

Now, of course, when the wife of the late giant came down from the steeple, she was of her usual size, say fifty-five feet, seven and a quarter inches. But Prigio had been in so many dangers (which would have shaken a heart less brave), and was so grateful for his escape, and was thinking so much of so many things, including his beloved absent bride, that he was a little absent-minded himself. He quite forgot that the husband of the giant's wife had been reduced, by his own wish, to the height of an ordinary tall man.

When the restored wife saw Hexenhausen, who came up to her ankle or so, she gave a shriek, and Prigio feared that she would faint, and fall into his arms. Of course he might as well have tried to support a falling steeple as a lady nearly sixty feet in height!

Hexenhausen himself was obviously alarmed, and stood at a safe distance from his spouse.

Fortunately, the alert mind of Prigio perceived the remedy. He promptly wished that Madame von Hexenhausen might be five feet seven inches high, and that her clothes might continue to fit her. This happened.

The reunited pair then rushed into each other's arms, kissing beneath the fragrant lime-trees of the avenue.

Prigio rode on in front, and gave orders that the apartments of Madame von Hexenhausen should be prepared, and that her daughter should there await her long lost mother.

Then the prince looked at his fairy watch.

It marked *Present Times. Bed Time.*

The Crab that Played with the Sea

RUDYARD KIPLING

BEFORE the High and Far-Off Times, O my Best Beloved, came the Time of the Very Beginnings; and that was in the days when the Eldest Magician was getting Things ready. First he got the Earth ready; then he got the Sea ready; and then he told all the Animals that they could come out and play. And the Animals said, 'O Eldest Magician, what shall we play at?' and he said, 'I will show you.' He took the Elephant – All-the-Elephant there was and said, 'Play at being an Elephant,' and All-the-Elephant-there-was played. He took the Beaver – All-the-Beaver there was and said, 'Play at being a Beaver,' and All-the-Beaver-there-was played. He took the Cow – All-the-Cow-there-was and said, 'Play at being a Cow,' and All-the-Cow-there-was played. He took the Turtle – All-the-Turtle-there-was and said, 'Play at being a Turtle,' and All-the-Turtle-there-was played. One by one he took all the beasts and birds and fishes and told them what to play at.

But towards evening, when people and things grow restless and tired, there came up the Man (with his own little girl-daughter?) – Yes, with his own best-beloved little girl-daughter sitting upon his shoulder, and he said, 'What is this play, Eldest Magician?' And the Eldest Magician said, 'Ho, Son of Adam, this is the play of the Very Beginning; but you are too wise for this play.' And the Man saluted and said, 'Yes, I am too wise for this play; but see that you make all the Animals obedient to me.'

Now, while the two were talking together, Pau Amma the Crab, who was next in the game, scuttled off sideways and stepped into the sea, saying to himself, 'I will play my play alone in the deep waters, and I will never be obedient to this son of Adam.' Nobody saw him go away except the little girl-daughter where she leaned on the Man's shoulder. And the play went on till there were no more Animals left without orders; and the Eldest Magician wiped the fine dust off his hands and walked about the world to see how the Animals were playing.

He went North, Best Beloved, and he found All-the-Elephant-there-was digging with his tusks and stamping with his feet in the nice new clean earth that had been made ready for him.

'*Kun?*' said All-the-Elephant-there-was, meaning, 'Is this right?'

'*Payah kun,*' said the Eldest Magician, meaning, 'That is quite right'; and he breathed upon the great rocks and lumps of earth that All-the-Elephant-there-was had thrown up, and they became the great Himalayan Mountains, and you can look them out on the map.

He went East, and he found All-the-Cow-there-was feeding in the field that had been made ready for her, and licked her tongue round a whole forest at a time, and swallowed it and sat down to chew her cud.

'*Kun?*' said All-the-Cow-there-was.

'*Payah kun,*' said the Eldest Magician; and he breathed upon the bare patch where she had eaten, and upon the place where she had sat down, and one became the great Indian Desert, and the other became the Desert of Sahara, and you can look them out on the map.

He went West, and he found All-the-Beaver-there-was making a beaver-dam across the mouths of broad rivers that had been got ready for him.

'*Kun?*' said All-the-Beaver-there-was.

'*Payah kun,*' said the Eldest Magician; and he breathed upon

the fallen trees and the still water, and they became the Ever-glades in Florida, and you may look them out on the map.

Then he went South and found All-the-Turtle-there-was scratching with his flippers in the sand that had been got ready for him, and the sand and the rocks whirled through the air and fell far off into the sea.

'*Kun?*' said All-the-Turtle-there-was.

'*Payah kun,*' said the Eldest Magician; and he breathed upon the sand and the rocks, where they had fallen in the sea, and they became the most beautiful islands of Borneo, Celebes, Sumatra, Java, and the rest of the Malay Archipelago, and you can look *them* out on the map!

By and by the Eldest Magician met the Man on the banks of the Perak River, and said, 'Ho! Son of Adam, are all the Animals obedient to you?'

'Yes,' said the Man.

'Is all the Earth obedient to you?'

'Yes,' said the Man.

'Is all the Sea obedient to you?'

'No,' said the Man. 'Once a day and once a night the Sea runs up the Perak River and drives the sweet-water back into the forest, so that my house is made wet; once a day and once a night it runs down the river and draws all the water after it, so that there is nothing left but mud, and my canoe is upset. Is that the play you told it to play?'

'No,' said the Eldest Magician. 'That is a new and a bad play.'

'Look!' said the Man, and as he spoke the great Sea came up the mouth of the Perak River, driving the river backwards till it overflowed all the dark forests for miles and miles, and flooded the Man's house.

'This is wrong. Launch your canoe and we will find out who is playing with the Sea,' said the Eldest Magician. They stepped into the canoe; the little girl-daughter came with them; and the man took his *kris* – a curving, wavy dagger with a blade like a flame – and they pushed out on the Perak River. Then the Sea began to run back and back, and the canoe was sucked out of the mouth of the Perak River, past Selangor, past Malacca, past Singapore, out and out to the Island of Bintan, as though it had been pulled by a string.

Then the Eldest Magician stood up and shouted, 'Ho! beasts, birds, and fishes, that I took between my hands at the Very Beginning and taught the play that you should play, which one of you is playing with the Sea?'

Then all the beasts, birds, and fishes said together, 'Eldest Magician, we play the plays that you taught us to play – we and our children's children. But not one of us plays with the Sea.'

Then the Moon rose big and full over the water, and the Eldest Magician said to the hunchbacked old man who sits in the Moon spinning a fishing-line with which he hopes one day to catch the world, 'Ho! Fisher of the Moon, are you playing with the Sea?'

'No,' said the Fisherman, 'I am spinning a line with which I shall some day catch the world; but I do not play with the Sea.' And he went on spinning his line.

Now there is also a Rat up in the Moon who always bites the old Fisherman's line as fast as it is made, and the Eldest Magician said to him, 'Ho! Rat of the Moon, are *you* playing with the Sea?'

And the Rat said, 'I am too busy biting through the line that this old Fisherman is spinning. I do not play with the Sea.' And he went on biting the line.

Then the little girl-daughter put up her little soft brown arms with the beautiful white shell bracelets and said, 'O Eldest Magician! when my father here talked to you at the Very Beginning, and I leaned upon his shoulder while the beasts were being taught their plays, one beast went away naughtily into the Sea before you had taught him his play.'

And the Eldest Magician said, 'How wise are little children who see and are silent! What was that beast like?'

And the little girl-daughter said, 'He was round and he was flat; and his eyes grew upon stalks; and he walked sideways like this; and he was covered with strong armour upon his back.'

And the Eldest Magician said, 'How wise are little children who speak truth! Now I know where Pau Amma went. Give me the paddle!'

So he took the paddle; but there was no need to paddle for the water flowed steadily past all the islands till they came to the place called Pusat Tasek – the Heart of the Sea – where the great hollow is that leads down to the heart of the world, and in that hollow grows the Wonderful Tree, Pauh Janggi, that bears the magic twin-nuts. Then the Eldest Magician slid his arm up to the shoulder through the deep warm water, and under the roots of the Wonderful Tree he touched the broad back of Pau Amma the Crab. And Pau Amma settled down at the touch, and all the Sea rose up as water rises in a basin when you put your hand into it.

'Ah!' said the Eldest Magician. 'Now I know who has been playing with the Sea'; and he called out, 'What are you doing, Pau Amma?'

And Pau Amma, deep down below, answered, 'Once a day and once a night I go out to look for my food. Once a day and once a night I return. Leave me alone.'

Then the Eldest Magician said, 'Listen, Pau Amma. When you go out from your cave the waters of the Sea pour down into Pusat Tasek, and all the beaches of all the islands are left bare, and the little fish die, and Raja Moyang Kaban, the King of the Elephants, his legs are made muddy. When you come back and sit in Pusat Tasek, the waters of the Sea rise, and half the little islands are drowned and the Man's house is flooded, and Raja Abdullah, the King of the Crocodiles, his mouth is filled with the salt water.'

Then Pau Amma, deep down below, laughed and said, 'I did not know I was so important. Henceforward I will go out seven times a day, and the waters shall never be still.'

And the Eldest Magician said, 'I cannot make you play the play you were meant to play, Pau Amma, because you escaped me at the Very Beginning; but if you are not afraid, come up and we will talk about it.'

'I am not afraid,' said Pau Amma, and he rose to the top of the sea in the moonlight. There was nobody in the world so big as Pau Amma – for he was the King Crab of all Crabs. Not a common Crab, but a King Crab. One side of his great shell touched the beach at Sarawak; the other touched the beach at Pahang; and he was taller than the smoke of three volcanoes! As he rose up through the branches of the Wonderful Tree he tore off one of the great twin-fruits – the magic double-kernelled nuts that make people young – and the little girl-daughter saw it bobbing alongside the canoe, and pulled it in and began to pick out the soft eyes of it with her little golden scissors.

'Now,' said the Magician, 'make a Magic, Pau Amma, to show that you are really important.'

Pau Amma rolled his eyes and waved his legs, but he could only stir up the Sea, because, though he was a King Crab, he was nothing more than a Crab, and the Eldest Magician laughed.

'You are not so important after all, Pau Amma,' he said. 'Now, let *me* try,' and he made a Magic with his left hand – with just the little finger of his left hand – and, lo and behold, Best Beloved, Pau Amma's hard, blue-green-black shell fell off him as a husk falls off a cocoa-nut, and Pau Amma was left all soft – soft as the little crabs that you sometimes find on the beach, Best Beloved.

'Indeed, you are very important,' said the Eldest Magician. 'Shall I ask the Man here to cut you with his *kris*? Shall I send for Raja Moyang Kaban, the King of the Elephants, to pierce you with his tusks? or shall I call Raja Abdullah, the King of the Crocodiles, to bite you?'

And Pau Amma said, 'I am ashamed! Give me back my hard shell and let me go back to Pusat Tasek, and I will only stir out once a day and once a night to get my food.'

And the Eldest Magician said, 'No, Pau Amma, I will *not* give you back your shell, for you will grow bigger and prouder and stronger, and perhaps you will forget your promise, and you will play with the Sea once more.'

Then Pau Amma said, 'What shall I do? I am so big that I can only hide in Pusat Tasek, and if I go anywhere else, all soft as I am now, the sharks and the dogfish will eat me. And if I go to Pusat Tasek, all soft as I am now, though I may be safe, I can never stir out to get my food, and so I shall die.' Then he waved his legs and lamented.

'Listen, Pau Amma,' said the Eldest Magician. 'I cannot make you play the play you were meant to play, because you escaped me at the Very Beginning; but if you choose, I can make every stone and every hole and every bunch of weed in all the seas a safe Pusat Tasek for you and your children for always.'

Then Pau Amma said, 'That is good, but I do not choose yet. Look! there is that Man who talked to you at the Very Beginning. If he had not taken up your attention I should not have grown tired of waiting and run away, and all this would never have happened. What will *he* do for me?'

And the Man said, 'If you choose, I will make a Magic, so that both the deep water and the dry ground will be a home for you and your children – so that you shall be able to hide both on the land and in the sea.'

And Pau Amma said, 'I do not choose yet. Look! there is

that girl who saw me running away at the Very Beginning. If she had spoken then, the Eldest Magician would have called me back, and all this would never have happened. What will *she* do for me?'

And the little girl-daughter said, 'This is a good nut that I am eating. If you choose, I will make a Magic and I will give you this pair of scissors, very sharp and strong, so that you and your children can eat cocoa-nuts like this all day long when you come up from the Sea to the land; or you can dig a Pusat Tasek for yourself with the scissors that belong to you when there is no stone or hole near by; and when the earth is too hard, by the help of these same scissors you can run up a tree.'

And Pau Amma said, 'I do not choose yet, for, all soft as I am, these gifts would not help me. Give me back my shell, O Eldest Magician, and then I will play your play.'

And the Eldest Magician said, 'I will give it back, Pau Amma, for eleven months of the year; but on the twelfth month of every year it shall grow soft again, to remind you and all your children that I can make magics, and to keep you humble, Pau Amma; for I see that if you can run both under the water and on land, you will grow too bold; and if you can climb trees and crack nuts and dig holes with your scissors, you will grow too greedy, Pau Amma.'

Then Pau Amma thought a little and said, 'I have made my choice. I will take all the gifts.'

Then the Eldest Magician made a Magic with the right hand, with all five fingers of his right hand, and lo and behold, Best Beloved, Pau Amma grew smaller and smaller and smaller, till at last there was only a little green crab swimming in the water alongside the canoe, crying in a very small voice, 'Give me the scissors!'

And the girl-daughter picked him up on the palm of her little brown hand, and sat him in the bottom of the canoe and gave him her scissors, and he waved them in his little arms, and opened them and shut them and snapped them, and said, 'I can eat nuts. I can crack shells. I can dig holes. I can climb trees. I can breathe in the dry air, and I can find a safe Pusat Tasek under every stone. I did not know I was so important. *Kun?*' (Is this right?)

'*Payah kun*,' said the Eldest Magician, and he laughed and gave him his blessing; and little Pau Amma scuttled over the side of the canoe into the water; and he was so tiny that he could have hidden under the shadow of a dry leaf on land or of a dead shell at the bottom of the sea.

'Was that well done?' said the Eldest Magician.

'Yes,' said the Man. 'But now we must go back to Perak, and that is a weary way to paddle. If we had waited till Pau Amma had gone out of Pusat Tasek and come home, the water would have carried us there by itself.'

'You are lazy,' said the Eldest Magician. 'So your children shall be lazy. They shall be the laziest people in the world. They shall be called the Malazy – the lazy people'; and he held up his finger to the Moon and said, 'O Fisherman, here is this Man too lazy to row home. Pull his canoe home with your line, Fisherman.'

'No,' said the Man. 'If I am to be lazy all my days, let the Sea work for me twice a day for ever. That will save paddling.'

And the Eldest Magician laughed and said, '*Payah kun*' (That is right).

And the Rat of the Moon stopped biting the line; and the Fisherman let his line down till it touched the Sea, and he pulled the whole deep Sea along, past the Island of Bintang, past Singapore, past Malacca, past Selangor, till the canoe whirled into the mouth of the Perak River again.

'*Kun?*' said the Fisherman of the Moon.

'*Payah kun*,' said the Eldest Magician. 'See now that you pull the Sea twice a day and twice a night for ever, so that the Malazy fishermen may be saved paddling. But be careful not to do it too hard, or I shall make a Magic on you as I did to Pau Amma.'

Then they all went up the Perak River and went to bed, Best Beloved.

Now listen and attend!

From that day to this the Moon has always pulled the Sea up and down and made what we call the tides. Sometimes the Fisher of the Sea pulls a little too hard, and then we get spring-tides; and sometimes he pulls a little too softly, and then we get what are called neap-tides; but nearly always he is careful, because of the Eldest Magician.

And Pau Amma? You can see when you go to the beach, how all Pau Amma's babies make little Pusat Taseks for themselves under every stone and bunch of weed on the sands; you can see them waving their little scissors; and in some parts of the world they truly live on the dry land and run up the palm trees and eat cocoa-nuts, exactly as the girl-daughter promised. But once a year all Pau Ammas must shake off their hard armour and be soft – to remind them of what the Eldest Magician could do. And so it isn't fair to kill or hunt Pau Amma's babies just because old Pau Amma was stupidly rude a very long time ago.

Oh yes! And Pau Amma's babies hate being taken out of their little Pusat Taseks and brought home in pickle-bottles. That is why they nip you with their scissors, and it serves you right!

Prince Rabbit

A. A. MILNE

ONCE upon a time there was a King who had no children. Sometimes he would say to the Queen, 'If only we had a son!' and the Queen would answer, 'If only we had!' And then on another day he would say, 'If only we had a daughter!' and the Queen would sigh and answer, 'Yes, even if we had a daughter, that would be something!' But they had no children at all.

As the years went on and there were still no children in the Royal Palace, the people began to ask each other who would be the next King to reign over them. And some said that perhaps it would be the Chancellor, which was a pity, as nobody liked him very much; and others said that there would be no King at all, but that everybody would be equal. Those who were lowest of all thought that this would be a satisfactory ending of the matter; but those who were higher up felt that, though in some respects it would be a good thing, yet in other respects it would be an ill-advised state of affairs; and they hoped therefore that a young Prince would be born in the Palace. But no Prince was born.

One day, when the Chancellor was in audience with the King, it seemed well to him to speak what was in the people's minds.

'Your Majesty,' he said; and then stopped, wondering how best to put it.

'Well?' said the King.

'I have Your Majesty's permission to speak my mind?'

'So far, yes,' said the King.

Encouraged by this, the Chancellor resolved to put the matter plainly.

'In the event of Your Majesty's death . . .' He coughed and began again. 'If Your Majesty ever should die,' he said, 'which in any case will not be for many years – if ever – as, I need hardly say, Your Majesty's loyal subjects earnestly hope – I mean they hope it will be never. But assuming for the moment – making the sad assumption –'

'You said you wanted to speak your mind,' interrupted the King. 'Is this it?'

'Yes, Your Majesty.'

'Then I don't think much of it.'

'Thank you, Your Majesty.'

'What you are trying to say is, "Who will be the next King?"'

'Quite so, Your Majesty.'

'Ah!' The King was silent for a little. Then he said, 'I can tell you who won't be.'

The Chancellor did not seek for information on this point, feeling that in the circumstances the answer was obvious.

'What do you suggest yourself?'

'That Your Majesty choose a successor from among the young and the highly born of the country, putting him to whatever test seems good to Your Majesty.'

The King pulled at his beard and frowned.

'There must be not one test, but many tests. Let all, who will, offer themselves, provided only that they are under the age of twenty and are well born. See to it.'

He waved his hand in dismissal, and with an accuracy established by long practice the Chancellor retired backwards out of the Palace.

On the following morning, therefore, it was announced that all those who were ambitious to be appointed the King's successor, and who were of high birth and not yet come to the age of twenty, should present themselves a week later for the tests to which His Majesty desired to put them, the first of which was to be a running race. Whereat the people rejoiced, for they wished to be ruled by one to whom they could look up, and running was much esteemed in that country.

On the appointed day the excitement was great. All along the course, which was once round the Palace, large crowds were massed, and at the finishing point the King and Queen themselves were seated in a specially erected Pavilion. And to this Pavilion the competitors were brought to be introduced to Their Majesties. And there were nine young nobles, well built and handsome, and (it was thought) intelligent, who were competitors.

And there was also one Rabbit.

The Chancellor had first noticed the Rabbit when he was lining up the competitors, pinning numbers on their backs so that the people should identify them, and giving them such instructions as seemed necessary to him.

'Now, be off with you,' he had said. 'Competitors only, this way.' And he had made a motion of impatient dismissal with his foot.

'I am a competitor,' said the Rabbit. 'And I don't think it is usual', he added with dignity, 'for the starter to kick one of the competitors just at the beginning of an important foot-race. It looks like favouritism.'

'You can't be a competitor,' laughed all the young nobles.

'Why not? Read the rules.'

The Chancellor, feeling rather hot suddenly, read the rules. The Rabbit was certainly under twenty; he had a pedigree which showed that he was of the highest birth; and –

'And,' said the Rabbit, 'I am ambitious to be appointed the King's successor. Those were all the conditions. Now let's get on with the race.'

But first came the introduction to the King. One by one the competitors came up . . . and at the end –

'This,' said the Chancellor, as airily as he could, 'is Rabbit.

Rabbit bowed in the most graceful manner possible; first to the King and then to the Queen. But the King only stared at him. Then he turned to the Chancellor.

'Well?'

The Chancellor shrugged his shoulders.

'His entry does not appear to lack validity,' he said.

'He means, Your Majesty, that it is all right,' explained Rabbit.

The King laughed suddenly. 'Go on,' he said. 'We can always have a race for a new Chancellor afterwards.'

So the race was started. And the young Lord Calomel was much cheered on coming in second; not only by Their Majesties, but also by Rabbit, who had finished the course some time before, and was now lounging in the Royal Pavilion.

'A very good style, Your Majesty,' said Rabbit, turning to the King. 'Altogether he seems to be a most promising youth.'

'Most,' said the King grimly. 'So much so that I do not propose to trouble the rest of the competitors. The next test shall take place between you and him.'

'Not racing again, please, Your Majesty. That would hardly be fair to his Lordship.'

'No, not racing. Fighting.'

'Ah! What sort of fighting?'

'With swords,' said the King.

'I am a little rusty with swords, but I daresay in a day or two –'

'It will be now,' said the King.

'You mean, Your Majesty, as soon as Lord Calomel has recovered his breath?'

The King answered nothing, but turned to his Chancellor.

'Tell the young Lord Calomel that in half an hour I desire him to fight with this Rabbit –'

'The young Lord Rabbit,' murmured the other competitor to the Chancellor.

'To fight with him for my Kingdom.'

'And borrow me a sword, will you?' said Rabbit. 'Quite a small one. I don't want to hurt him.'

So, half an hour later, on a level patch of grass in front of the Pavilion, the fight began. It was a short, but exciting struggle. Calomel, whirling his long sword in his strong right arm, dashed upon Rabbit, and Rabbit, carrying his short sword in his teeth, dodged between Calomel's legs and brought him toppling. And when it was seen that the young Lord rose from the ground with a broken arm, and that with the utmost gallantry he had now taken his sword in his left hand, the people cheered. And Rabbit, dropping his sword for a moment, cheered too; then he picked it up and got entangled in his adversary's legs again, so that again the young Lord Calomel crashed to the ground, this time with a sprained ankle. And there he lay.

Rabbit trotted to the Royal Pavilion, and dropped his sword in the Chancellor's lap.

'Thank you so much,' he said. 'Have I won?'

And the King frowned and pulled at his beard.

'There are other tests,' he muttered.

But what were they to be? It was plain that Lord Calomel was in no condition for another physical test. What, then, of an intellectual test?

'After all,' said the King to the Queen that night, 'intelligence is a quality not without value to a ruler.'

'Is it?' asked the Queen doubtfully.

'I have found it so,' said the King, a little haughtily.

'Oh,' said the Queen.

'There is a riddle, of which my father was fond, the answer to which has never been revealed save to the Royal House. We might make this the final test between them.'

'What is the riddle?'

'I fancy it goes like this.' He thought for a moment, and then recited it, beating time with his hand.

> 'My first I do for your delight.
> Although 'tis neither black nor white.
> My second looks the other way,
> Yet always goes to bed by day.
> My whole can fly, and climb a tree,
> And sometimes swims upon the sea.'

'What is the answer?' asked the Queen.

'As far as I remember,' said His Majesty, 'it is either "dormouse" or "raspberry".'

'"Dormouse" doesn't make sense,' objected the Queen.

'Neither does "raspberry",' pointed out the King.

'Then how can they guess it?'

'They can't. But my idea is that young Calomel should be secretly told beforehand what the answer is, so that he may win the competition.'

'Is that fair?' asked the Queen doubtfully.

'Yes,' said the King. 'Certainly, or I wouldn't have suggested it.'

So it was duly announced by the Chancellor that the final test between the young Lord Calomel and Rabbit would be the solving of an ancient riddle-me-ree, which in the past had baffled all save those of Royal Blood. Copies of the riddle had been sent to the competitors, and in a week from that day they would be called upon to give their answers before Their Majesties and the full Court. And with Lord Calomel's copy went a message, which said this:

'From a friend. The answer is "dormouse". BURN THIS.'

The day came round; and Calomel and Rabbit were brought before Their Majesties; and they bowed to Their Majesties, and were ordered to be seated, for Calomel's ankle was still painful to him. And when the Chancellor had called for silence, the King addressed those present, explaining the conditions of the test to them.

'And the answer to the riddle', he said, 'is in this sealed paper, which I now hand to my Chancellor, in order that he shall open it, as soon as the competitors have told us what they know of the matter.'

The people, being uncertain what else to do, cheered slightly.

'I will ask Lord Calomel first,' His Majesty went on. He looked at his Lordship, and his Lordship nodded slightly. And Rabbit, noticing that nod, smiled suddenly to himself.

'Lord Calomel,' said the King, 'what do you consider to be the best answer to this riddle-me-ree?'

The young Lord Calomel tried to look very wise, and he said:

'There are many possible answers to this riddle-me-ree, but the best answer seems to me to be "dormouse".'

'Let someone take a note of that answer,' said the King; whereupon the Chief Secretary wrote down 'Lord Calomel – "dormouse".'

'Now,' said the King to Rabbit, 'what suggestion have you to make in this matter?'

Rabbit, who had spent an anxious week inventing answers each more impossible than the last, looked down modestly.

'Well?' said the King.

'Your Majesty,' said Rabbit with some apparent hesitation, 'I have a great respect for the intelligence of the young Lord Calomel, but I think that in this matter he is mistaken. The answer is not, as he suggests, "woodlouse", but "dormouse".'

'I said "dormouse",' cried Calomel indignantly.

'I thought you said "woodlouse",' said Rabbit in surprise.

'He certainly said "dormouse",' said the King coldly.

'"Woodlouse", I think,' said Rabbit.

'Lord Calomel – "dormouse",' read out the Chief Secretary.

'There you are,' said Calomel, 'I did say "dormouse".'

'My apologies,' said Rabbit, with a bow. 'Then we are both right, for "dormouse" it certainly is.'

The Chancellor broke open the sealed paper, and to the amazement of nearly all present read out, 'dormouse'.

'Apparently, Your Majesty,' he said in some surprise, 'they are both equally correct.'

The King scowled. In some way which he didn't quite understand, he had been tricked.

'May I suggest, Your Majesty,' the Chancellor went on, 'that they be asked now some question of a different order, such as can be answered, after not more than a few minutes' thought, here in Your Majesty's presence. Some problem in the higher mathematics for instance, such as might be profitable for a future King to know.'

'What question?' asked His Majesty, a little nervously.

'Well, as an example – "What is seven times six?" ' And, behind his hand, he whispered to the King, 'Forty-two.' Not a muscle of the King's face moved, but he looked thoughtfully at the Lord Calomel. Supposing his Lordship did not know.

'Well?' he said reluctantly. 'What is the answer?'

The young Lord Calomel thought for some time, and then said, 'Fifty-four.'

'And you?' said the King to Rabbit.

Rabbit wondered what to say. As long as he gave the same answers as Calomel, he could not lose in the encounter, yet in this case 'forty-two' was the right answer. But the King, who could do no wrong, even in arithmetic, might decide, for the purposes of the competition, that 'fifty-four' was an answer more becoming to the future ruler of the country. Was it, then, safe to say, 'forty-two'?

'Your Majesty,' he said, 'there are several possible answers to this extraordinarily novel conundrum. At first sight the obvious solution would appear to be "forty-two". The objection to this solution is that it lacks originality. I have long felt that a progressive country such as ours might well strike out a new line in the matter. Let us agree that in future seven sixes are fifty-four. In that case the answer, as Lord Calomel has pointed out, is "fifty-four". But if Your Majesty would prefer to cling to the old style of counting, then Your Majesty and Your Majesty's Chancellor would make the answer "forty-two".'

After saying which, Rabbit bowed gracefully, both to Their Majesties and to his opponent, and sat down again.

The King scratched his head in a puzzled sort of way.

'The correct answer', he said, 'is, or will be in the future, fifty-four.'

'Make a note of that,' whispered the Chancellor to the Chief Secretary.

'Lord Calomel guessed this at his first attempt; Rabbit at his second attempt. I therefore declare Lord Calomel the winner.'

'Shame!' said Rabbit.

'Who said that?' cried the King furiously. Rabbit looked over his shoulder, with the object of identifying the culprit, but was apparently unsuccessful.

'However,' went on the King, 'in order that there should be no doubt in the minds of the people as to the absolute fairness with which this competition is being conducted, there will be one further test. It happens that a King is often called upon to make speeches and exhortations to his people, and for this purpose the ability to stand evenly upon two legs for a considerable length of time is of much value to him. The next test, therefore, will be –'

But at this point Lord Calomel cleared his throat so loudly that the King had to stop and listen to him.

'Quite so,' said the King. 'The next test, therefore, will be held in a month's time, when his Lordship's ankle is healed, and it will be a test to see who can balance himself longest upon two legs only.'

Rabbit lolloped back to his home in the wood, pondering deeply.

Now there was an enchanter who lived in the wood, a man of many magical gifts. He could (it was averred by the countryside) extract coloured ribbons from his mouth, cook plum-puddings in a hat, and produce as many as ten silk handkerchiefs, knotted together, from a twist of paper. And that night, after a simple dinner of salad, Rabbit called upon him.

'Can you,' he said, 'turn a rabbit into a man?'

'I can,' he said at last, 'turn a plum-pudding into a rabbit.'

'That,' said Rabbit, 'to be quite frank, would not be a helpful operation.'

'I can turn almost anything into a rabbit,' said the enchanter with growing enthusiasm. 'In fact, I like doing it.'

Then Rabbit had an idea.

'Can you turn a man into a rabbit?'

'I did once. At least I turned a baby into a baby rabbit.'

'When was that?'

'Eighteen years ago. At the court of King Nicodemus. I was giving an exhibition of my powers to him and his good Queen. I asked one of the company to lend me a baby, never thinking for a moment that ... The young Prince was handed up. I put a red silk handkerchief over him, and waved my hands. Then I took the handkerchief away ... The Queen was very much distressed. I tried everything I could, but it was useless. The King was most generous about it. He said that I could keep the rabbit. I carried it about with me for some weeks, but one day it escaped. Dear, dear!' He wiped his eyes gently with a red silk handkerchief.

'Most interesting,' said Rabbit. 'Well, this is what I want you to do.' And they discussed the matter from the beginning.

A month later the great Standing Competition was to take place. When all was ready, the King rose to make his opening remarks.

'We are now,' he began, 'to make one of the most interesting tests between our two candidates for the throne. At the word "Go!" they will –' And then he stopped. 'Why, what's this?' he said, putting on his spectacles. 'Where is the young Lord Calomel? And what is that second rabbit doing? There

was no need to bring your brother,' he added severely to
Rabbit.

'I am Lord Calomel,' said the second rabbit meekly.

'Oh!' said the King.

'Go!' said the Chancellor, who was a little deaf.

Rabbit, who had been practising for a month, jumped on
his back paws and remained there. Lord Calomel, who had
had no practice at all, remained on all fours. In the crowd at
the back the enchanter chuckled to himself.

'How long do I stay like this?' asked Rabbit.

'This is all very awkward and distressing,' said the King.

'May I get down?' said Rabbit.

'There is no doubt that the Rabbit has won,' said the
Chancellor.

'Which rabbit?' cried the King crossly. 'They're both
rabbits.'

'The one with the white spots behind the ears,' said Rabbit
helpfully. 'May I get down?'

There was a sudden cry from the back of the hall.

'Your Majesty!'

'Well, well, what is it?'

The enchanter pushed his way forward.

'May I look, Your Majesty?' he said in a trembling voice.
'White spots behind the ears? Dear, dear! Allow me!'

He seized Rabbit's ears and bent them this way and that.

'Ow!' said Rabbit.

'It is! Your Majesty, it is!'

'Is what?'

'The son of the late King Nicodemus, whose country is
now joined to your own. Prince Silvio.'

'Quite so,' said Rabbit airily, hiding his surprise. 'Didn't
any of you recognize me?'

'Nicodemus had only one son,' said the Chancellor, 'and
he died as a baby.'

'Not died,' said the enchanter, and forthwith explained the whole sad story.

'I see,' said the King, when the story was ended. 'But of course that is neither here nor there. A competition like this must be conducted with absolute impartiality.' He turned to the Chancellor. 'Which of them won the last test?'

'Prince Silvio,' said the Chancellor.

'Then my dear Prince Silvio –'

'One moment,' interrupted the enchanter excitedly. 'I've just thought of the word. I knew there were some words you had to say.' He threw his red silk handkerchief over Rabbit, and cried, 'Hey Presto!' and the handkerchief rose and rose and rose . . .

And there was Prince Silvio!

You can imagine how loudly the people cheered. But the King appeared not to notice that anything surprising had happened.

'Then, my dear Prince Silvio,' he went on, 'as the winner of this most interesting series of contests, you are appointed successor to our throne.'

'Your Majesty,' said Silvio, 'this is too much!' And he turned to the enchanter and said, 'May I borrow your handkerchief for a moment? My emotion has overcome me!'

So on the following day, Prince Rabbit was duly proclaimed heir to the throne before all the people. But not until the ceremony was over did he return the enchanter's handkerchief.

'And now,' he said to the enchanter, 'you may restore Lord Calomel to his proper shape.'

And the enchanter placed his handkerchief on Lord Calomel's head, and said, 'Hey presto!' and Lord Calomel stretched himself and said, 'Thanks very much!' But he said it rather coldly, as if he were not really very grateful.

So they all lived happily for a long time. And Prince Rabbit married the most beautiful Princess of those parts; and when a son was born to them there was much feasting and jollification. And the King gave a great party, whereat minstrels, tumblers, jugglers and such-like were present in large quantities to give pleasure to the company. But in spite of a suggestion made by the Princess, the enchanter was not present.

'But I hear he is so clever,' said the Princess to her husband.

'He has many amusing inventions,' replied the Prince, 'but some of them are not in the best of taste.'

'Very well, dear,' said the Princess.

Epilogue

The Magician Prospero bids farewell to his Magic Arts

Ye elves of hills, brooks, standing lakes, and groves;
And ye that on the sands with printless foot
Do chase the ebbing Neptune, and do fly him
When he comes back; you demi-puppets that
By moonshine do the green sour ringlets make,
Whereof the ewe not bites; and you whose pastime
Is to make midnight mushrumps, that rejoice
To hear the solemn curfew; by whose aid –
Weak masters though ye be – I have bedimm'd
The noontide sun, call'd forth the mutinous winds,
And 'twixt the green sea and the azure vault
Set roaring war: to the dread-rattling thunder
Have I given fire, and rifted Jove's stout oak
With his own bolt: the strong-based promontory
Have I made shake; and by the spurs pluck'd up
The pine and cedar: graves, at my command
Have waked their sleepers, oped, and let 'em forth
By my so potent Art. But this rough Magic
I here abjure; and, when I have required
Some heavenly music – which even now I do, –
To work mine end upon their senses that
This airy charm is for, I'll brake my staff,
Bury it certain fathoms in the earth,
And deeper than did ever plummet sound
I'll drown my book.

William Shakespeare: *The Tempest*, Act V, Sc. I.

Notes on Sources

EXCEPT in the case of the tale from Chaucer, I have myself retold all the myths, legends, fairy tales and romances in the first three sections of this book from the various sources indicated below. I have tried to present them as accurately as possible, adding nothing but some dialogue when this was lacking and seemed necessary; but I have omitted freely where stories were too long, and often cut incidents that had no direct bearing on the part which concerned a Magician.

Invitation: From *The Sorcerer* (1877) by W. S. Gilbert, Act One.

Teta the Magician: From the Westcar Papyrus (now in Berlin) written between 2000 and 1785 B.C. (Reprinted with minor alterations from *Tales of Ancient Egypt*, 1967, retold by Roger Lancelyn Green.)

A Hittite Charm against a Wizard's Spell: Freely versified from the prose translation given on p. 347 of *Ancient Near Eastern Texts Relating to the Old Testament*, edited by James B. Pritchard, 1955.

The Magician from Corinth: Combined from Apollodorus *The Library*, Book III, Section iii; Hyginus Fable CXXXVI and the fragments of the play *Polyidus* by Euripides.

The Sorcerer's Apprentice: Retold from Lucian's *Philopseudes* section 33–6. Lucian of Samosata, one of the greatest of the later Greek writers, lived from about A.D. 120 to 170.

Virgilius the Magician: Retold from the Medieval Romance of 'Virgilius' which was based on early Italian popular tales current in Naples.

Aladdin and the African Magician: Retold and shortened from 'The Story of Aladdin, or The Wonderful Lamp' in Galland's version of *Arabian Nights' Entertainments*, 15th English edition, 1779.

Merlin the Wizard of Britain: Combined and retold from Nennius, *History of the Britons*, sections 40–42; Geoffrey of Monmouth's *British History*, Book VI, Chapters 17–19 and Book VIII, Chapters 10–12 and 19–20; several passages from Layamon's *Brut* and Wace's *Roman de*

Brut, and Robert de Boron's *Merlin*. The adventures with Niviene are taken from the Medieval French *Suite de Merlin*.

Bradamante and the Wizard: Adapted freely from Lodovico Ariosto's *Orlando Furioso* (1532), Cantos II–IV.

The Franklin's Tale: Retold from Chaucer's *Canterbury Tales* (1377–1400) by Eleanor Farjeon in her *Tales from Chaucer* (1930).

The Magician's Horse: Retold from the version from *Sicilianische Märchen* given in *The Grey Fairy Book* (1900).

The Gifts of the Magician: Retold from the version from *Finnische Märchen* given in *The Crimson Fairy Book* (1903).

The Magician's Pupil: Retold from the Danish fairy tale 'Master and Pupil' given in *The Pink Fairy Book* (1897).

The Magician who Had no Heart: Retold from the version from *Cuentos Populars Catalens* given in *The Pink Fairy Book* (1897).

The Wizard King: Adapted from the French 'Court Fairytale' in *Les Fées Illustres*, the fifth volume of *Le Cabinet des Fées*, 41 volumes (1785–9).

Chinook and Chinok: This poem by Andrew Lang is based on a tale in Charles Marelle's *Le Petit Monde* (1863). Lang's poem was published in *Longmans' Magazine*, August 1888, collected in his *Poetical Works* (1923), Vol. III, pages 176–7.

The Castle of Kerglas: This was first published in *Le Foyer Breton* (1845) by Emile Souvestre (1806–54) and is based on a folktale. The present version is that by Mrs Andrew Lang from *The Lilac Fairy Book* (1910).

The Magician and his Pupil: This story by Frau Amelie Linz-Godin first appeared in the English version given here in the *Strand Magazine*, May 1897, and was collected in *The Diamond Fairy Book* (a collection of similar stories from the *Strand*, with illustrations by H. R. Millar).

The Magicians' Gifts and *The Magician Turned Mischief-maker*, by Juliana Horatia Ewing (1841–85), first appeared in *Aunt Judy's Magazine*, March 1872 and November 1876, and were collected in her *Old-Fashioned Fairy Tales* (1882).

The Princess and the Cat, by E. Nesbit (1858–1924), first appeared in *The Jabberwock*, October 1905, and was collected in her *Oswald Bastable – and Others* (1905).

The Magician who Wanted More, by Andrew Lang (1844–1912) was published in his last book of original fairy stories, *Tales of a Fairy Court* (1906).

The Crab that Played with the Sea, by Rudyard Kipling (1865–1936), first appeared in *Pearson's Magazine*, August 1902, and was collected in *The Just So Stories* (1902).

Prince Rabbit, by A. A. Milne (1882–1956), first appeared in *Number Two Joy Street*, Blackwell's children's annual for 1923.

Epilogue: Prospero's speech from Act V, Scene 1, lines 32–57, of *The Tempest* (1611) by William Shakespeare (1564–1616).

Acknowledgements

THE Editor and Publishers are indebted to the following for permission to include copyright material in this book:

The Bodley Head Ltd, London, and Henry Z. Walck, Inc., New York, for permission to include *Teta the Magician* from TALES OF ANCIENT EGYPT by Roger Lancelyn Green, © Roger Lancelyn Green 1947; Oxford University Press for permission to include *The Franklin's Tale* from TALES FROM CHAUCER by Eleanor Farjeon; John Farquharson Ltd on behalf of the Estate of E. Nesbit for permission to include *The Princess and the Cat* from OSWALD BASTABLE AND OTHERS; Mrs George Bambridge and the Macmillan Companies of London and Canada, and Doubleday & Company, Inc., New York, for permission to include *The Crab that Played with the Sea* from THE JUST SO STORIES by Rudyard Kipling; Curtis Brown Ltd, London, on behalf of the Estate of A. A. Milne, and E. P. Dutton & Co., Inc., New York, for permission to include *Prince Rabbit* from NUMBER TWO JOY STREET by A. A. Milne (American title PRINCE RABBIT AND THE PRINCESS WHO COULD NOT LAUGH, © 1966 by Dorothy Daphne Milne and Spencer Curtis Brown).

The Editor and Publishers have made every effort to trace the holders of copyright in all extracts included in this anthology. If any query should arise, it should be addressed to the Publishers, and if it is found that an error has been made it will be corrected in future editions.

Also in Puffins

HEARD ABOUT THE PUFFIN CLUB?

... it's a way of finding out more about Puffin books and authors, of winning prizes (in competitions), sharing jokes, a secret code, and perhaps seeing your name in print! When you join you get a copy of our magazine, *Puffin Post*, sent to you four times a year, a badge and a membership book.

For details of subscription and an application form, send a stamped addressed envelope to:

The Puffin Club Dept A
Penguin Books Limited
Bath Road
Harmondsworth
Middlesex UB7 ODA

and if you live in Australia, please write to:

The Australian Puffin Club
Penguin Books Australia Limited
P.O. Box 257
Ringwood
Victoria 3134